Zaylie

A Passover Story

W. H. Rosenthal

Lynn & Hazel
for all the fine meals
we've shared
and for all those to come
Bill

Chapbook Press

Schuler Books
2660 28th Street SE
Grand Rapids, MI 49512
(616) 942-7330
www.schulerbooks.com

Zaylie – A Passover Story

ISBN 13: 9781943359363

Library of Congress Control Number: 2016940158

Printed in the United States by Chapbook Press.

In gratitude to Richard G. Stern

And, of course, Isaac Babel

"Remember when we were slaves in Egypt…"
from the Passover Haggadah

"And in our own time remember. Always remember." the Vitebsker Rebbe, translated from the Yiddish

Mah nishtanoh halaila hazeh mikol ha'leilot
Wherefore is this night different from all other
nights?

The Dream

The dream begins as it always begins, with the
pounding at the door, interrupting her father's
reading of the Haggadah. He holds the matzo high
for all to see: "This is the bread of affliction…"

The pounding at the door overwhelms the sound of
his voice. The blows are crushing, as though
breaking down the door is more important than
announcing a presence. It is unlike anything she has
ever heard. Everyone looks to the door. There is a
moment of total silence frozen in her memory. It is
a black and white photograph which exists only in
her mind and will always be there, and when she is
gone, it will be gone. She hears the wood screaming
as it shatters. Then the scene speeds up, like a
movie run amok, and in an instant her father is on

his feet and around the table, behind her. She remembers things, the sound of the matzo as it shattered in his hands and how his hands feel as he grabs her by the shoulders and shoves her toward the back of the apartment. "Zaylie", he says, "Run!" It is a whisper and a shout all at once. It is the last word she remembers ever hearing from her father. Every year Jews all over the world sit around the Seder table reading from the Passover Haggadah and they ask this question:

Mah nishtanoh halaila hazeh mikol ha'leilot, why is this night different from all other nights? Such a simple question this "Why"?

Why?

For Zaylie it is not so simple, for it is the night Zaylie always dreams the dream. It is the only night of the year Zaylie dreams the dream. On all other nights she might dream of her beloved dog, Muttke. Or she might dream of her father, a man who loved to make jokes. People would ask what kind of dog

Muttke was, when it should have been clear to anyone that she carried within her the bloodlines of every breed of dog which had ever walked the earth since Noah first hit dry land. "She is a Norwegian Short-Haired Poodle," he would answer very seriously, causing Zaylie to clap her hand over her mouth. She had been taught that it was not polite to laugh at people. Or she might dream of her mother, a good woman who gave her life over to making it possible for her husband to devote himself to his patients. But on this night she would dream of the dark cramped space at the top of the stairwell where she hid, listening to the shrieks of fear and the cries of pain and finally the silence. She does not remember how she ran from there, as her father had commanded, but she remembers the orange stripe on the streetcar, the face of the stranger who pulls her onto the moving platform, hundreds of images, always there in the dream.

Zaylie dreams the same dream every year on erev Pesach. The dream begins with the pounding on the

door. At first she is running from the Seder table.
The dream does not explain how she escapes the
building, nor how she runs from the streetcar when
it reaches the end of its line. Dreams are like that,
aren't they? It is night and there is fog. She is still
running, through the woods, now out of the city,
aware somehow that someone has told her to run,
that someone has shoved her through the back door
and under the steps, hiding just as she remembers
doing as a child, and she can hear the sounds of the
soldiers in the distance and the sounds of the dogs
even nearer. She runs faster and faster, but the
sounds of the dogs grow closer. Her legs are like
logs and her lungs scream to her that they are on
fire, but she runs on and on and on until she
collapses almost gratefully against the saw toothed
bark of a tree so large she thinks she can hide
behind in the way she did in delightful games of
hide and seek.

On any other night she might have dreamt of her
brother, who teased her and was often petulant with
her but who held her hand if she was frightened

when their parents were away for an evening. It was
her father who turned Rachel into Razela, but it was
her brother who turned Razela into Zaylie. In her
heart, she would always be Zaylie. It was her
brother's thin voice she remembered all her life as
he chanted the questions: *Ma Nishtana...*
Wherefore is this night different?

For a long time, she pressed her face into the
dream-bark, sobbing as she drew in the air as best
she could, even as her lungs screamed for more.
You owe us this air, Zaylie, they shout, and then
they scream "More! More!" And with each scream
they claw at her chest. After an eternity her body
stops heaving, her lungs quiet, and she regains
control of her legs; only then she pulls her face from
the tree and turns to face the dogs.

On any other night she might dream of her mother
and the way her mother brushed her hair before
bedtime, first a hundred strokes, then the fussing
with a curl, finally the hand which smooths

something out of place only a mother can see. "Oh, mother," she would say, pretending to be exasperated, and then they would both laugh and hug each other and it would be time for bed.

There are perhaps twelve of them, maybe more. She recognizes them from the book about dogs in her father's library, in the bookcase with the leaded glass doors. They are Dobermans, big black creatures, a coppery bow on each chest, feet marked with the same copper, ears butchered when they were babies and canted forward, sharp, like knives, stubs for tails, huge chests, slender waists. They have encircled her and are panting easily. They, too, have run fast and hard, but they were made for this, and their chests do not heave in fiery agony. Each is pointed toward her, head slightly lowered, neck arched down, hair rippling along the spine. Everything about them says to Zaylie that this is the end, that she will be ripped apart by these creatures from hell. Zaylie is not very old, maybe thirteen, maybe fourteen, but she can see that this is the end.

She is surprised to be so calm.

One of the dogs moves to approach her. The others move not at all. The dog approaches slowly, not yet showing teeth, not yet snarling, but as though it has not decided what it will do. It is observing Zaylie and her responses. Zaylie tries to turn away, unwilling to stare into the fiery eyes of death, but she cannot move.

The great beast speaks: "I am the leader. I am Mitzi". Zaylie does not how she can understand the dog, nor does she have the sense that this is a dream. Mitzi sniffs the air near Zaylie and moves closer. "Wait," she says to the pack. The other dogs are still, standing ready, waiting. Mitzi has made no sound, yet her words are clear to Zaylie. In the dream Zaylie does not find it strange that she understands. Mitzi sniffs at Zaylie's shoe, then moves slowly up the child's leg to the knee, touching the delicate blonde hairs from time to time. Zaylie shrinks back into the bark, waiting for

the terrible pain which must come. The dog pauses.
"This" Mitzi says, her head turned toward the circle
of dogs, "is Muttke's Zaylie." To Zaylie's eyes, the
dogs show no response to this news. Their eyes
glow, lit by the fires of hell. Even the sounds of
their breathing are frightening, each inhalation a
snarl, each exhalation a threat.

Mitzi sniffs her way up Zaylie's legs, lingering here
and there. Zaylie's arms hang limp at her sides, and
the great dog moves her nose around them, taking in
information and reporting to the others. "Muttke
says that Zaylie has been a good servant and even
when food became scarce always shared from her
own plate... Muttke says that she never went
without food even when the rest of that pack was
hungry."

Mitzi raised her head and sniffed the air and paused.
"I sense that Muttke is gone now," she said without
sadness, just reporting a fact, "but she has left us
messages to tell us that Zaylie was under her

protection and asks that we honor this." As one, the dream Dobermans sit, each one like the next, sculpted from fog and night. Zaylie cannot move, paralyzed as one is often paralyzed in dreams, yet she does not feel fear. This surprises her.

In the distance behind the dogs, Zaylie can see the soldiers. They are no longer running. Are they tired, too? No matter. They press on. She is too tired to run again, and she resigns herself again to her death. She thinks her family must be dead by now. Why should she not join them?

Mitzi says, "Come, Zaylie, we must leave now. We cannot send the soldiers away, but we will do what we can to honor Muttke's wish."

"I can run no more." Zaylie is not sure whether she says this or thinks it, but Mitzi seems to understand.

"Do the best you can," says Mitzi. Zaylie does the best she can, walking quickly through her pain in a direction the dogs herd her. Two of the dogs run to the left, and they bark and snarl as dogs might in hell. It is a harsh and frightening sound made worse by the horrible rasp of their breathing. Some of the soldiers, their long gray coats dragging heavily through the wet underbrush, follow. Two of the dogs run to the right, and some of the soldiers follow, their long gray coats dragging them down as they slog through the wet underbrush. Even though dogs leave the pack again and again to distract the soldiers, Zaylie is sure that there are never fewer dogs escorting her. She doesn't understand how this can be, but she accepts it. There are always soldiers behind them, cursing, shouting, snarling. Sometimes she can hear the sound of a rifle and the high pitched snarl of the bullet as it snaps through the woods.

For fifty years or more the dream has ended at the railway station. Somehow they have eluded the soldiers. She does not know what town this is; it could be any. The dogs take her to the end of a line of children and elderly men and women who are being loaded on a cattle car. She looks into the dogs' eyes and sees sadness there, and then they are gone. This is always the dream. It is always the same.

But tonight the dream is different. *Mah nishtanoh halaila hazeh*?

The dogs are still there. Zaylie becomes alert. Her ears pick up. Zaylie becomes aware of things she has never noticed in the dream. She sniffs at the air and takes in the smells of the place, the oil and steam and coal soot of the trains, the fear-smell of the children in the line in front of her, the stink of the soldiers' damp and sweaty coats. A soldier, an officer perhaps, immaculate in his uniform, handsome like a movie star. "Come children, this way," he says. We are going to Pitchi Poi, the children's village. It is lovely there, and you will have toys to play with and sweet things to eat. Come. Don't be afraid. Come. And the line of children moves forward.

But now the dream is changing, different. *Mah nishtanoh halaila hazeh?*

Tonight Mitzi tells her "It is time for you to come with us Zaylie." And Zaylie, understanding, grateful, turns and runs with the dogs.

Tales from the Shtetl

And then it was erev Pesach again. The table was
set for thirty-two. Of course that was too large for
the dining room, which could seat no more than
sixteen with all the leaves in the table. The staff
from Katz's Kosher Katering had carefully moved
tables to the living room and leveled them so well
that, with the tablecloths in place, it all looked like
one very long table. Silver Seder plates alternated
with floral arrangements from "Zaidelstein's
Unique Floral" in matching silver vases every few
places so that no guest might feel neglected.
Some of the living room furniture had been in the
way. The 1932 Ampico Grand, Irving's prized
antique player piano, had been moved closer to the
front wall. There was a piano roll on the Ampico
playing Yiddish melodies during the meal, the ghost
hands of Horowitz skimming across the keyboard.
The club chairs which normally lived in front of the
fireplace had been put in the study next to the huge

color projection TV. A sideboard had gone to the study. Otherwise, the room had absorbed the tables well.

Last year, first Seder was at the Ross's. Next year it would be at the Bernstein's. The year after that at the Garber's' then the Ross's again, and the year after that it would be back here at the Meijer's. The Haggadahs were always the same; they traveled to the correct house each year in an old fashioned leather briefcase case dedicated to that task. It belonged to Irv's father.

The food was much the same. Good. Traditional. After all, how many ways are there for the same caterer to make matzo ball soup? One year they had tried building the Seder around a rather nice, rather French menu: potage parmentier, tournedos, a sort of matzo based tart tatin, but it had not seemed quite right, even though the food had been very, very good, better than the usual stuff, they had all agreed. So they went back to what their mothers and grandmothers had served, gefilte fish ("god help us all, those women had actually made the gefulte fish"), matzo ball soup, roasted chicken, kugel. You know.

The other senior partners and their wives were there. As always there were assorted relatives and offspring, some married, some still in law school, one trying to find acting work in New York and worrying his parents, a cousin or two and their kids. Irv's father and mother were away this year. There was a special Seder at the Jewish War Veterans Museum in Washington. All the surviving liberators would be there to honor some general. Irv had heard the name, but it meant nothing to him. At their end of the table, the partners were playing their traditional ending of the Seder meal game of trying to top each other's family stories. They called it tales from the shtetl, the shtetl being the old Dexter/Davison neighborhood in Detroit, before everyone moved farther and farther northwest until they finally moved right out of the city and into the synagogue suburbs. Near the middle of the table, the Chasid from New Jersey, who was Irv's son in-law, and Billy, his nephew, an internist from

Champaign-Urbana, were debating all the nuances of the words which translated from the Yiddish as "whore". Each year the Chasid tells his wife that they cannot go to Detroit, that he cannot eat in a house that isn't kosher enough. Each year she tells him that she will take care of everything, their own tablecloth, their own dishes, their own food brought with them from New Jersey. Each year when they have returned to New Jersey and thrown away the tablecloth and the dishes, she asks "now that wasn't so bad was it?" And each year he nods his head and says "Well, after all, we are all lawyers, so the conversation is good."

No one else knew why this particular conversation had started, nor did anyone else pay any attention to it. Before the evening would end, each of the debaters would have at least one dictionary of Yiddish and one of Hebrew at hand as the discussion continued. Their wives, who had heard all this or something just like it before, were discussing the exhibit of Impressionists at the DIA and whether there would be time to go tomorrow and whether that would cause a fight with the Chasid. Near the far end of the table Irv's cousin from Milwaukee and one of the junior members of the firm were engaged in passionate discussion of what the achievement of the one gigahertz processor and the four terabyte hard drive would mean for their next home computer acquisitions. From somewhere along the table, bubbles of talk about the lack of archeological evidence that the Israelites had been anywhere near Egypt in the time of the building of the pyramids floated above the other conversations like speech balloons floating over a cartoon table. No one else appeared to pay attention to this discussion. For that matter, no one seemed to pay attention to any discussion more than two people removed.

Other talk bubbles floated up and down the table "… and then the female rabbi and the female cantor ran off together to Denver, and we had to start another rabbi search …I mean we are a liberal congregation after all, but that was just a little more liberal than…" "… and then there's some Jewish gun nut in Milwaukee with a web-site. Says we should all arm ourselves. Can you imagine? Jews with guns? I mean, really…"

Scattered among these clusters of adults were a few children and a pair of teenagers with their own bubble bath of words. And there was Zaylie, who had lived with the Meijers family since the end of the War. To them she was aunt Rachel, but she knew who she was. She was Zaylie.

She ate very little, but seemed to enjoy the traditional dishes, nodding her head and murmuring as each arrived. She wore, as she did every day of Irving's memory, a white blouse, perfectly pressed, with a high collar and long sleeves, carefully buttoned at the wrist. No one at this table was quite sure exactly how Zaylie came to live with the Meijers. She had been a part of their lives since she had come to America after the War, before any of them were born, a survivor of the camps, a relative on his dad's side, Irv thought, but exactly what the relationship was he couldn't remember, and you couldn't exactly ask her. He thought that his father had found her somehow during the war or, perhaps, right after, and he made a mental note to ask when Max called from Washington after the veterans' Seder was over. However it happened, he thought, it must have taken a miracle to find a relative in one of the prison camps.

Actually, you could ask Zaylie anything, and she would seem to answer, but in the end, you knew no more than when you had first asked. It wasn't that her English was so poor that it was hard to talk with her, although her English was still, after all these years, heavily accented. Rather, it was that she was so often somewhere else. Somewhere from which she seemed unable to return in order to pay much attention to what others were saying. She took care of herself, minded the children when they were young -- first Irv and his sister, and then his kids-- talked quite unobtrusively to herself, and, in spite of her arthritis gnarled hands, cross-stitched rather

lovely pieces, some of which his father had framed
and hung first in his house, then at his father's
request in Irv's house when the big house Irv grew
up in had been closed up for much of the year while
Max and Mindy spent the cold Michigan winters
drifting around interesting places. Max had said "I
think it will make her feel at home when she stays
with you while we're away." One of her pieces, a
scene from Little Red Riding Hood, the wolf, dark
and rather graceful, with pointed ears and an oddly
short tail, trailing along after the young girl, hung
over the family room fireplace. Behind them were
fir trees lovely and green. The wolf looked more
like a big old dog than a creature to be feared. When
he was young, Irving had once asked her about the
wolf's unnaturally short tail. Zaylie just shrugged
and looked at her hands, as if to say "With hands
like these, what could you expect?"

If you paid attention, you could see that the Pesach
napkins were hers, too, each with scenes from the
Exodus stitched in the corners in incredibly fine
needlework The table was full save for the one

place for Elijah, the Prophet, of course.

That some of the stories had been heard around the Seder table since they were children at their parents' Seders seemed to make little difference to anyone at the partners' end of the table. They were much like the stories in the Hagadah, annual and familiar, an important part of the ritual. They were like the matzo crumbs that fell to the table when the Haggadahs were opened, a reminder of other years.

Irving had the privilege of leading off this year, because the Seder was at his house, the house he and Mindy had built on the lake after they sold the house in Indian Village. He was telling the story of how his grandfather, taking chicken soup made by his mother to his sick brother in Flint, which was a long way from Dexter Avenue in those days. "She had made him promise to take his Model A and deliver the soup." Irv warms to the telling of this story. "When the steam poured out of the engine about halfway there he stopped the car and having no water he pours the chicken soup into the radiator.

When he arrives in Flint he drains the chicken soup back into its pot and refills the radiator. Now here's the kicker. When the brother tastes the soup, he says it is the best their mother ever made. My grandfather swore that he never said a word about this while his wife lived."

"Now, gather round all you shleppers" Bernstein jumps in before anyone else can get started "and listen to this. Here, there's a true story, and this one is not wearing a beard. A man comes into the office the other day to draw up a pre-nup. Right? His name is Hersh Bernstein, so I say to him that I doubted we were related, but I'd tell him what I knew about my family. So he holds up his hand like a traffic cop. So I stop and wait. So he says that he appreciates the thoughtfulness but I shouldn't bother because Bernstein is not his real family name. When his grandfather came to this country, the family name was something like Czyswatkowkzya, or something equally unpronounceable, and he wanted an American name for his new life in America. He wanted to be a real

American, so he changed it to Bernstein." Whether it was the wine or the warmth from the fireplace Irv's thoughts had begun to drift. He went from a story about Moses to thoughts of people he had seen when he visited the seniors' home with his B'nai Brith group and wondered about an old man with a great white beard. How soon before he was that old? He drank too much of the sweet wine still in his glass and choked a bit on it. His hand, wine glass still in it, came up automatically and he bathed his shirt and the tablecloth in Mogen David. As he mopped at the table and his shirtfront, he began to laugh and cough at the same time so violently he could not speak. He tried to regain control so that he could respond, but every time he tried to blurt out his retort, he laughed and sputtered again, which, in the aftermath of the meal and the wine, was contagious, of course. The rest of the table went in stages from concern to amusement to chuckling to roaring and rolling in their chairs watching him. No one knew what was so funny, it was just an epidemic of laughter. Only after they had all gone through one version or another of clutching at their sides in pain did the laughter, like a spring Mitzistorm, slow down, and subside in gasps of relief. "Oh, God," sighed Sylvia, "That was terrible. Sara" she said, "please go get a towel for this disaster." She pointed at her husband, indicating clearly that he was the disaster. Far down the table even Eric, who had read the Four Questions over his protests that he was now almost fourteen in a mix of the high pitch of a little boy and the struggling tones of a young adolescent trying, oh so, hard to lower his voice, shook his head as if to say "adults". He looked for a response from his sister, Madeleine, but at fifteen Madeleine found both the adults and her brother much too boring even when she agreed with him. She gave him the absolutely blank stare which said this isn't worth the energy to turn away.

The third partner, Sandy Ross, the one who lived in the house built by the younger of the Dodge brothers said, "Well, I can tell a true story about Oivy's family." He addressed this to his new wife.

One of the reasons he had divorced his first wife was that she didn't like these stories and would leave the room when they started. The new wife looked at him as he spoke the way his Labrador looked at a hand filled with steak. "You know how the name got to be Meijer, the same as the Meijer stores all over the state, the same as the Dutch Reform Meijers?

Everyone at that end of the table turned to look at him. Farther down the table, conversations continued and Madeleine looked off toward the corner above the window.

"When his great-grandfather got off the boat it was Meyer" Sandy waived an unlit cigar in punctuation to his lines. "When Oivy's grandfather started the law practice, Mendel, he was still Mendel Moishe Meyer then, Manny to friend and client alike. When someone would ask him if he was one of the Meijers from Grand Rapids, he would say no, he was one of the Meyers from Minsk. Now you have to understand that Manny was young, just married, and virtually penniless and desperate for clients, so one time when somebody asked, for a joke, he said sure. So the fellow said, that's good, I have a case for you. Well, it didn't take very long for Manny to figure out what was going on and as M. Maurice Meijer, Maury to all of his buddies, he developed the largest and most lucrative practice representing Dutch Reform businessmen outside of Grand Rapids. And that", he said, raising his wine glass as if in a toast, "is a fact, Jack".

Irving shrugged in defeat. "And to top it all off," he said, "they all knew my grandfather went to shul. Apparently the name was good enough." One year, a promising new attorney in the firm had suggested that the oddity of the spelling was likely no more than an error at Ellis Island. He was never again invited to one of the Seders, nor was it long before he decided to move to a practice in Toledo. Irving motioned for Eric to go open the door for Elijah, and Sara, looking very elegant in one of

Elaine's last year's dresses, passed around the table, filling the wine glasses, and clearing away the last of the dinner plates.

As Eric struggled to push his chair against the opposite push of the thick carpet to leave the table, there was a heavy thud at the door. Three times it was repeated. The air vibrated with the sound. All the conversations went silent. Eric stopped, half standing, hands braced on the table, and turned to look at his father.

Had any one looked at Zaylie, which no one did, he would have seen her go pale.

Szmul

Szmul was more than something of a puzzle to his parents. They knew that children, boys especially, reached an age of rebelling, trying to be something different from their parents. Although they were not particularly analytical, nor were they at all well read, they had seen this often enough among their circle of friends and fellow actors to be prepared for it. In fact, they rather hoped for it. To have a lawyer or, please, an accountant or agent in the family, someone they could trust would truly be a blessing. As the team of Bierstein and Wineglass, they played all the vaudeville stages of Europe with a comedy routine which was based in their abilities to mimic in comic form the accents of all the nations of Europe. Louis, no longer the Lebel his parents had named him, would open the act, say in Paris, dressed in oversized lederhosen kept from falling by a truly lurid set of Bavarian suspenders and a huge alpine hat pulled down over his ears and

with an enormous feather towering over both the hat
and Louis. "Helga", he would say in garbled
French with the worst possible mockery of a
German accent " Vat are dose noises on de roov?"
Rosalyn, whom her mother and father remembered
as Rivke, would answer slowly, patiently, and in an
impeccable version of French with the slightest of
accents as spoken by the most educated of Germans
"Those, my dear, are the elements."
To this Louis would throw up his hands and shout
"Vel tell dose elephants to get offen de rrrroof."
The audience would roar at the stupid German.

In Berlin, Louis was dressed in an immense beret, a
shirt purchased from the remains of a production of
the Three Musketeers, a red kerchief at the neck,
trousers much too short for his skinny legs,
revealing mismatched striped stockings. He would
say in German but in a travesty of a French accent
"Hildegarde, my leetle dove what can zis be on zee
roov, zose noises." At the punch line, following an
extravagantly Gallic shrug, "tell zeeze alefawnz to

get off ze roov", the German audiences would split
their sides over the stupid Frenchman. And so they
made their way around the theaters of Europe
making audiences at every stop on their itinerary
laugh at their cloddish neighbors. In the process,
they made a lot of money. Unfortunately, what they
didn't spend on lavish living went into the pockets
of their lawyers, agents, and accountants, hence
their hope that the boy would rebel against their
Bohemian life style by turning toward a practical
life. "Thieves!" Louis shouted in the dressing room
before and after each performance because there
were always money problems.

Like so many parental dreams for their children,
this was not to be. Samuel -- this pronounced by his
parents as though he had just arrived from studies at
the London School of Economics -- insisted on
calling himself Szmul after his grandfather. From
that gentleman, who had made a living trading in
currencies, Szmul had inherited a head for numbers,
especially incredibly quick calculations and an

almost intuitive sense of all the rules and nuances of geometry. From this grandfather, he inherited also a steady hand and a good eye. These gifts for which his parents had such high hopes, he turned into two trades: gambling at cards and gambling at billiards. And for his education he turned not to London and the School of Economics but to Paris and the school of billiard parlors and casinos and dance halls and cabarets and the beautiful, beautiful women of that wonderful world.

In that time of worldwide depression, he thought that he had years left ahead of him for school and the tedium of working. And although his parents did well, he could not imagine himself as an actor. A billiard player, yes. An actor, no thanks.

Zaylie

The apartment was large, housing her father's medical offices in the front as well as the very ample living quarters for the Doctor's family. The building dated from the late 1840's. Originally a single building, it had been joined later, in the 1860's or the 70's – the records were for some reason rather vague -- to its twin next door, at the rear by a stairwell and airshaft, at the front by a lobby and stairwell. The stairwell at the rear was rather nice, a circular stairwell with paintings on the landings, but it had one oddity. It didn't quite reach the fourth floor. The architect had cursed the builder, the builder cursed the architect. In the end, the builder solved the problem by extending the stairs to the right and to the left from where the original plans had appeared to stop, five steps up to the left, five to the right. The architect was furious, but there it was, and so it remained. "Like Hannibal crossing the Alps," the Doctor always said of the trip from the kitchen of the living quarters and the laboratory at the rear of the office. He had said it enough that Zaylie had begun to raise her eyebrows every time he said it, but she was sure to look away so that he didn't see. Laughing at her father, the Doctor, was unthinkable. Eventually her father had the stairs extended and the gap covered. He had the carpenter make a little secret, a doorway into the space newly covered over. He thought it might be a good place to hide a few presents, or a new cane whose price he didn't want to mention to his wife. Behind the lobby was a pleasant garden in the space between the original parts of the structure. Later, room was carved from the garden to make way for a small elevator. At street level were shops: a dealer in vintage books, a shop which sold miniatures for doll houses, a coffee house where one might also buy fine chocolates, and an art gallery. Above the shops were apartments, four to each side of the combined building. The nineteenth century became the twentieth; the building was wired first for electricity, then for the telephone. Otherwise it remained much the same. The wood panels of the lobby became darker with age. Once every few years the stairwells were re-carpeted or repainted. It was a well-maintained building. Their apartment ideal for the Doctor, part medical office, part residence. When the Doctor had taken these apartments for his practice and for his family life, he had this apartment joined the one next door, through the foyer at the front and through the family kitchen and to his small laboratory in the other. The Doctor's waiting room, paneled much like the entry way and the foyer in front of each apartment, was lined with shelves filled with books and his collections, which spilled over to display tables and cases also, and eventually to the sitting room. The Doctor collected many things: primitive masks and figures from Africa, figures carved by Indians from America -- he had been to America only once and had decided that it was truly interesting but not yet a very civilized or cultured place to live. Perhaps his grandchildren might live there, he had thought at the time, but it was not a place for him and his family --interesting mineralogical specimens, bones from many species, antique pocket watches, stamps from around the world arranged in bound volumes. But his greatest pleasure came from his collection of canes, which his wife said was probably the only reason Bortmann, the cane dealer, had made a living all these years. Most of these he kept in the living quarters so that he could be surrounded by them when he was at his leisure. His special love was the *canne système*, the 18th and 19th century walking sticks which concealed something, everything from a piano tuner's tools in the handle to a cunning stick which concealed within its shaft a fishing rod. He had sticks which held their owner's gloves, which concealed pencils and cigarettes or beautiful watches and compasses. He had sticks which cast shadows of political figures from times when the followers of those figures could not openly identify themselves and sticks which were designed to hold absinthe, and sticks to carry perfumes, and sticks whose handles were opera glasses. He had racks filled with sticks and umbrella stands filled with sticks and tables designed to hold billiard cues filled with sticks. He had a stick which was a playable violin and one which concealed the music stand for the violin player, but his collection included none of the often beautiful weapons sticks he found interesting but wrong. Their sword blades and daggers and pistols seemed to him inappropriate for a humanistic Jew, and he had thought of their potential danger for inquiring children. Early in his collecting days, he had decided that he would have none of them. For a long time, his friend Bortmann, the dealer in antique canes, tried again and again to tempt him with a poacher's cane. It was a brilliantly disguised single shot shotgun in French .42 caliber, which Bortmann had acquired once on a trip to Paris. The barrel was covered in a beautiful and incredibly thin maple veneer and gave a clue as to its real purpose to only the very well trained eye. "For shooting the King's deer," said Bortmann with a twinkle. "In these times maybe even for something else," Bortmann added, "since the Nazis came." The Doctor had been tempted by its beauty and incredibly ingenious design, but in the end, he stayed with his original decision. "To protect the little ones," he had said to Bortmann, "I cannot have this in the house."

 The bookseller was to the left of the entry, the maker of chocolates to the right. There are on this night eight boxes for mail , four on one side, four on the other, one for Slivkin the bookseller who is no longer there to sell books, one for the maker of chocolates whose kettles have not been touched since he was led away one day.: Slivkin, the bookseller whose shop doors were closed, Schroenburg, the professor of mathematics whom no one has seen for almost two months, Bortmann, the seller of antique canes and umbrellas, Gleuck who sold and repaired fine watches and who left a year ago in the hope of reaching New Jersey where his brother lived, the widow Mermel with her cats, who played her record player very softly all night long, and, of course, Zaylie's father, the Doctor.. Who could know where they were? After the Germans came, the shops closed one by one. They were, after all, owned by Jews.

The Seder

Tonight, as they waited for his wife to bring the Passover meal, such as it would be in these times, there was no talk of canes, only of "the situation". Slivkin and Bortmann with their wives and the widow Mermel, "the survivors" as Slivkin liked to say, and of course the Doctor and Madame and the two children. In the old days, there had always been twenty or more at the first Seder, relatives, friends, and always one or two who needed a meal. Now it was just those who were still in the building. The food was always wonderful in the old days. Now it was not even possible to find matzoth, so they did what they could to make their own as it had been made in the desert, rolling out flat bits of dough and baking them immediately until hard, dry flat pieces emerged from the oven. When the Nazis first came, a member of the Jewish Council, a longtime patient, had come to the Doctor and said that he would be safe because he was a physician. Although many of the Jewish community were being relocated in order to work in German industry, he would remain because a physician was very important, an asset to his community, someone the Germans needed. So said the member of the Jewish Council. Now, they sat at the Doctor's table, the nine of them, seven adults and two children, and each of the adults wondered if there would be another Seder here and, if so, how many would be at the table.

As they talk of the situation, there is a horrible pounding at the door. The sounds are crushing, as though the intention is to break down the door more than to announce a presence. It is unlike any sound Zaylie has ever heard. Everyone looks to the door but her father.

Another Seder

"Dad," Eric yelled from the door, "it's the police."
Irv looked at his guests, shrugged his shoulders, and
stood up, turned, went to the front door. "Go sit
down," he said to Eric.

"Mike," he said when he reached the doorway. It
wasn't the police but the subdivision's security
patrol. He could see the car in the street with only
its parking lights illuminated, its emergency lights
dark.

"Yes, sir, Mr. Meijer, I'm really sorry to bother you
on your holiday and all that, but I wanted to check.
There's a big stray dog, black, with no collar we
just picked up. I know it isn't yours, but I know
you have a lot of guests tonight and I wasn't on the
gate when they came in so I didn't know if it might
belong to one of your people. I didn't want to call
animal control until I was sure."

"Good idea, but I don't think so," Irv said. "Come
in for a minute. I'll ask just to be sure. Come on in,
and I'll be right back."

"Everybody, it's Mike, one of our subdivision's security guys. He wants to know if anyone here has lost a large, black dog."

Everyone seemed to relax, and conversations started up again. Everyone was talking, everyone but Zaylie.

When he returned to the foyer, Irv shook his head. "No, nobody here claims it." Irv shook the guard's hand and gave him a bottle of Chivas. "Thanks for asking, that was very kind of you."

"Thank you, Mr. Meijer." The security guard took the bottle in his left hand, touched the brim of his cap with the tips of the finger of his right hand and disappeared into the night.

Back at the table, Marty raised a hand and said "In the interest of ever getting to bed tonight, I hereby declare Sandy the winner of this year's contest. Now isn't there anyone else who noticed that Elijah came in with the cop? I don't know about the rest of you shleppers, but I have work to do in the morning. Someone has to pay the bills for this year's cruise." Conversation died out in waves down the long table, and Haggadahs reappeared.

Pinchus

His parents' disappointment began when Pinchus
was nine, though they did not know it until much
later. Then he had the nine-year old's sense of
discretion and diplomacy. By the time he was old
enough for his parents to think seriously about his
bar mitzvah, he had gone from simple questioning
to rebellious rejection of everything his father and
mother held dear. And yet he loved them for
reasons he would not understand for many years. At
nine, he was merely puzzled. He stood with his
father, who, like all the men in the prayer house
wrapped himself in a tallis the size of a Bedouin
warrior's cloak, welcome enough on a cold, damp
morning in the unheated room that was their
synagogue. In those days, all stood through the
prayers. There were, of course, the benches and
chairs the students used at cheder, but they were
shoved to the walls or against the shelves stuffed
with books cascading in every possible direction.
In front of them were the ark with its two precious

torahs and the reader's table. Oh, yes, let us not forget the buckets and the pots and pans. These were placed strategically to contain each of the 10 leaks in the roof, a minyan of leaks his father had said, as he maneuvered himself and the boy to a prime position near the ark but between the miserable, cold, streams, worse as the gray spring wore on. The rain came down and the prayers floated up, in their accustomed order. During the special, seasonal prayers, the boy's attention, until then somewhat adrift in the hypnotic buzz and hum and swaying of the devout, returned to the prayer book. The letters shifted back into focus to make words, and the words clustered to make ideas. They were praying for rain! "Rain!" he thought. Here, there was nothing but rain for weeks. They were drowning in rain. The streets were flooded and the river swollen with the stuff. The prayer house smelled of the wet rot from it. His mind was now fully alert, standing now at full attention, if you will. While his father, like the other men, raced on toward the concluding prayers, he read and reread those few lines again and again. He was transfixed. He put his hand out, held it under the heavy drops of the nearest leak until it was completely wet and cold. "Rain?" something in his mind screamed at him. "Why are we praying for rain?"

He almost did the unthinkable and tugged at his father's sleeve while the old man continued his prayers, lost in them, unaware that in this moment his son had changed forever, unaware that his dreams would never be his son's dreams. From then until the Germans led him to the shower room, he understood his son less and less every day.

Billiards Mouffetard

The Passage Jouffroy was a wonderful place for a young man. It was a glass ceiling arcade built during the 1800's, perpendicular to the very busy Boulevard Montmartre in order to circumvent the laws which taxed business on the basis of the size of their windows facing the street. Half way down the passage from the street, past shops filled with exotica, pastry shops, and cafes was the Hotel Chopin. The passage bent around the hotel for another half a block or more, this part filled with sellers of books, all kinds of books, new books, antique books, art books, books filled with Art Nouveau, or impressionists, or surrealists, and on and on. It was a place full of theater people. The Chopin was clean and respectable. It had the best croissants in all of France at the breakfast table, and the price was agreeable, as was the staff.
Szmul was well known in all of these shops and stores. After all, he had grown up here during the

times his parents played the Paris stage. He was a very pretty child and people remembered him, and the women of these places clucked over him each time he returned, commenting on how much he had grown, how good looking he was, how some had a daughter. He was greeted with the courtesy reserved for a good customer, no, for a good and entertaining customer whose French, very good but not quite perfect, was offered with enthusiasm and an accent the shopkeepers and waitresses and barmen all found charming. Szmul could do any accent he wanted in at least five languages, and he found that this one served him well. Clearly, now that he had reached his teens, the waitresses found it especially charming.

There were enough billiard parlors on this side of the river and on the Left Bank, too, that he could almost always find someone who thought he could beat Szmul the Sharpshooter, a nickname he relished. And now and then someone did beat him. Or perhaps more accurately, now and then he lost a match for a few francs. But in the big money matches, he always seemed to come out on top, often coming from behind at the very end to win by just a few points. He always talked about how lucky he had been to beat such a masterful opponent when he thought that the match was as good lost. And he always thanked his opponent and spoke of hoping to have the privilege of playing him again as he bought drinks for everyone before he pocketed his winnings. One fine early spring night, sitting on the Boulevard Montmartre at his favorite sidewalk table at the café Zephyr, next to the passage, sipping the house champagne, he was approached by a large man with a well-trimmed beard, a Yank by his accent, but his French was good. He asked if he might sit down. Szmul nodded. "D'accord" he said.

The man ordered a cognac. When it came, he asked "Are you the fellow they call the Sharpshooter?" Szmul nodded, amused. It was like the American Westerns he loved to watch at the Rex or the Max Linder in the streets just to the east of the passage. He could tell that he was about to be challenged, and it amused him. The American should have ordered a shot of red-eye. He laughed when Szmul told him that. "Have you been to the West" the man asked, surprised.

"No" said Szmul. Amsterdam is the farthest west I have ever been, but I feel that I know it well from the movies. I love the gunfighters. I go to watch the cowboy and Indian club in the Tuilleries, but I'll never know that life. Paris, Warsaw, Berlin, those are my places, the civilized places. But you have business. What may I do for you?" Szmul the Sharpshooter loved this part, and he sat cool and relaxed, waiting for the challenge.

"I play billiards over in the fifth sometimes, at the "Billiards Mouffetard" on the Rue Mouffetard near the Place Contrescarpe. Do you know the neighborhood?"

Szmul played with his champagne the way a movie gunfighter would play with this whiskey. "Yes" he said. "Down two flights of stairs, I think. Not a bad place. They keep the tables in pretty good shape. What time? What stakes?"

"Let's say after supper, around 10, tomorrow if you like. Three rail. Call your shots. A thousand francs a game?" Not a lot of boys, for he was certainly not quite yet a man, could shrug casually about such stakes, but he had won a lot of money at billiards. By the time they had played through the night, entire choirs of spectators had come and gone. Around midnight, when he was up fifteen thousand, Szmul admitted that he knew who his opponent was and addressed him as Mr. Hemingway when he asked if he wished to continue. "Yes" said the American "This is fine. I have never played anyone this good. It's fine to play, even to lose when you are playing the very best you can play against someone who is playing with brilliance." He paused, chalked his cue, and then asked "You knew all along who I am"?

"Yes, sir."

"How did you know?" He swirled the balls, the two white and the one red on the green felt, then placed them for a fresh start. He signaled for another round of cognac for himself and Szmul and everyone watching the match.

"I saw your picture in the bookstores."

Hemingway smiled and nodded.

Sometime after six in the morning, when Szmul was ahead fifty thousand francs, Hemingway said "This has been fine, but my eyes are giving out. I think that's enough for me, but I'd like a rematch." He went to the coats hanging on hooks on the wall, took his wallet from the inside pocket of the Harris Tweed jacket he had dropped on the floor when he first came in. During the night, someone hung it up. The wallet had not been touched. He counted out his losses in large bills.

Szmul stuffed the money into the pocket of his trousers, tasting the roll of bills with his fingers. "Of course I'll give you a rematch, but you'd better bring lots of money." They both laughed at his brass.

As they climbed the stairs to the street level, they could hear the bells of St. Medards, farther down the Rue Mouffetard, telling the hours.

When they reached the street, they stopped for a

moment to listen. Then Hemingway gestured to the right, toward the Place Contrescarpe. "Come on. Breakfast is on me. We can stop at La Chope. The food's so-so, but the beer is good."

As they ate, Hemingway asked the boy if he knew what was going on in Spain.

"Yes, sir." Szmul said. "It's in the papers. There is going to be some kind of civil war."

"Well," said Hemingway, "I'm going to go down there to see firsthand, but I think it's going to be more than a civil war in Spain. Before it's done, all of Europe will be up in flames. You ever think about moving to the states?" Szmul shook his head. "Well, think about it. It won't be long before Europe isn't going to be a good place for anyone." That were quiet for a while. Hemingway looked at Szmul. "You ever go shooting in the Loire?"

"No, sir, I've only played the tables here in Paris." Hemingway roared with laughter: "No, no" he said, "bird shooting, and anybody who can take that much money from me can stop calling me sir. Come on, we'll take a few days before I go to Spain, and

I'll teach you to shoot. You never know when it might come in handy."

When he returned to the Chopin from three days of bird shooting, Szmul found a note from his mother dated the previous day:

"Dear Samuel,

Karskifky (the goniff, may his agent's heart turn to slime) has bookings for us in Berlin and Warsaw. We must leave this afternoon. Meet us in Berlin at the Hotel Bathsheba."

It was signed "Your loving mother." In the envelope was some money and a ticket to Berlin. He laughed at the idea that his mother thought he needed money.

When he left for the Gare de Lyon, and the train for Berlin, he winked at lovely dark-haired Anna, the day clerk at the Chopin on Wednesdays and Fridays. "Wait for me sweetheart" he said. "I won't be away long."

Zaylie

Her father moves faster than she has ever seen. He grabs her by her shoulders and shoves her toward he back of the apartment. "Run", he says, "Hide in the stairs until they are gone". It is a whisper and a shout all at the same time. They are the last words she remembers ever hearing from her father. For the rest of her life, from that moment until she is on the train, she can remember nothing. How she came to escape from the apartment, from the building, from the city, all that is lost to her. Her life ends as her father's words die out, and a different life begins somewhere else.

Irv

Irv's office had become something of an unintentional shrine to his efforts within the Jewish community. Every plaque he had ever received with a gavel mounted on it, each one with the tablets of the ten commandments, every bronzed plate noting his leadership, which of course meant fundraising, every photograph with other recipients of mounted gavels, tablets, and bronzed plates, every photograph with a visiting Israeli official, every photograph with the national leaders of important organizations, and, of course, every photograph with an elected official, Democrats of course, and even a few Republicans. Three walls of the office were covered with them, the relentless work of Harriet, his secretary. He had even tried throwing out some of them, but she found the stack and back they went. First time visitors to his office were stunned with the recognition that here was someone very important. If the sheer volume did not do the job for a prospective client, the framed front page of the New York Times with Irv and President Clinton in deep discussion in the Oval Office took care of any possible lingering doubts. Irv, however, had not actually looked at them in years, not even the new ones. What he did look at was the wall beside his desk. This bit of wall space he had claimed for his own, several times over if the truth be told, in spite of Harriet's perseverance. There was nothing on it but a series of needlework pictures, each piece a portrait of the engine and each of the cars of a train, something Aunt Rachel had made for his room when he was a boy.

Had you asked him, Irv would have said that he had never thought a lot about her, and, yet, there was something about her that was never far from his mind, an image which hovered just outside the part of him which dealt with the outside world, as though he had awakened from a dream in which she had played some important but impossible to remember role, as it often is with dreams. She was always just there, had always been just "there", a part of the family in Detroit. Well, that's not exactly right. As a boy, he had often thought to ask her about her life before the war, what it was like, what her family was like. "Oh," she would say. "That's too long ago and too far away for me to remember. If I remember some time, I'll tell you." He had been nine or ten at the time he first thought to ask and filled with a sense of curiosity about life and all its details. He waited for a while for her to remember, but that didn't seem to happen, and in the whirlpool of other important questions overwhelming his mind, he would forget about it, or at least let it go until his curiosity overwhelmed him again. Her answers were always about the same, and by the time he was in college, he had stopped asking.

When he was growing up in his father's house -- he always thought of it as his father's-- although, he supposed, it was his mother's too. His mother, Mindy, was a good person, and he loved her with an appropriate loyalty, but she was a busy, busy person. While his father, Max, made the law firm and Irv and Irv's sister his life, his mother made causes hers. If there were funds to be raised, whether it be for a new building for the congregation or the JCC, or for the State of Israel, or for Hadassah Hospital, or the cancer research unit at Wayne State, his mother would be chairwoman or, as times changed but his mother did not, chairperson. Now, at an age when most people had long since retired from paid work, she was chair of the Jewish Welfare Federation's annual campaign. Sometimes he wondered if he had married Sylvia because she too was a master fund raiser and represented something of his mother in a way that was more accessible to him. A generation earlier Mindy had chaired the capital campaign to build a new Hillel building at the U of M. Now Sylvia was chairing a campaign to build an even newer Hillel building. Irv thought that the U of M needed a new building only because Michigan State had recently built one said to actually outshine the one at U of M. But nothing so trivial as a lack of real need could stop his wife any more than it could have stopped his mother. If the old building weren't named the Mindy Meijer Hillel at U of Michigan, Irv thought, it would only be because Max had given enough money to the university that it could have changed its name to the University of Mindy. He doodled on his desk pad "The Mindy Hillel at the University of Mindy" followed by "The New Sylvia Hillel (formerly the Mindy Hillel) at the University of Mindy: a daughter in law's tribute to her mother-in-law." He wondered how their fund raising efforts would compare in constant dollars and then began to wonder if either actually believed more in those causes or in fund raising. He had often thought that it was what he -- and they -- had instead of real religious faith, every dollar raised a kind of prayer. He envied believers. There were times when he lusted after faith, but he could not find it. He made fun of what he saw as the Chasid's superstitious beliefs, but deep within himself, he recognized that the Chasid, delusional or not, had something he did not. He had never spoken of this to anyone, nor could he imagine ever doing so. His parents had traveled all those years of his

growing up. Back and forth they went to Israel.
Back and forth they went to California and Arizona
and Florida at first and then to France and Spain and
on and on. During all those childhood and growing
up years, it was Aunt Rachel who had stayed at
home to take care of him and Rebecca. He had
often heard his father offer to take Aunt Rachel
along, but she always declined. "No," she would
say, in that funny sad way of hers. "I'll be here with
the *kinder*. Better I should stay here. They need
me." His parents cruised around the world, and
Aunt Rachel stayed at home with Irv and Rebecca.
Sometimes he thought that she was his real family
but that he knew nothing about her. It was a train of
thought that lead him nowhere but in a circle, back
to how much they had needed her.
And they did need her. It was to her they went to
when there was a scrape or scratch and the need for
a band aid. It was her they sought to cure a
heartbreak whether a broken toy or, later,
adolescent love unrequited.
It was her handwork, the needlepoint pieces she

stitched with such care and patience for them, which they added to whatever was the décor of the moment, dolls for Rebecca, cars for Irv. When Rebecca was a little girl, her Aunt Rachel made a beautiful piece of very fine stitching, which stayed on Rebecca's dressing table until she went to live in the South Quadrangle at the U of M. Then it lived in her room in the residence hall until she and Marcy Goldman left the residence hall for an apartment, and it lived in the apartment until she graduated. It was a lovely piece. It showed a pretty little girl in a flouncy dress and a soft brimmed hat. She is standing in a garden, looking over the fence at a picturesque little village in the distance. There are tiny clusters of flowers in the corners, and at the girl's feet is a small dog with a ribbon around its neck. Rebecca loved the little scene and was comforted by just the thought of it through those moments when she just knew that life had been harsh to her.

For Irving's room, it was a train. The engine, and

then each car, was a separate piece. Max had them framed, and they hung in order, the little engine puffing white smoke. The cars had windows, and the countryside behind them was beautiful, a shifting scene of lush green forests and rolling farmlands. A stream ran through several of the panels. One of the panels showed a child waiting, watching the car, perhaps hoping that the train would stop for a moment so that the child could get on, or so it seemed to Irv. He had loved this piece above all the rest and had moved it to his office, where it hung to the side of his desk.

Studying it often lead to thoughts about her hands, the joints knotted with arthritis, and he shook his head at his sense of the pain it must have cost her to make these beautiful gifts for them. For a while his mind drifted, trying to imagine where the train was going, and his head began to nod. He snapped himself upright and turned his attention to the case on his desk, a tricky bit of autoworker's compensation, which could, if all went well, bring the firm a substantial fee, a very substantial fee.

Pinchus

For Pinchus the love of learning was so intense that
he never said a word to his parents about his utter
lack of belief lest they remove him from the cheder.
It met in the same room in which prayers were held,
the desks and tables shoved back into place. It was
hot in summer, cold in winter, dry when not raining,
wet when it was raining. Not even the sounds of the
drops hitting the buckets and pots nor the dullness
of his teacher could distract Pinchus. To read from
the Torah was for him a course in history. He
learned quickly that to question the teacher about
what happened to history after Biblical times was
fruitless. "The history of the Jews is in three places:
the Torah, the Torah, and the Torah," said his
teacher, a grey bearded old man in dusty frock coat
and a huge black yarmulke, just before smacking
him across the hand with a stick. "Learn that, and
you will need no more. Learn it well enough and
some day you will be permitted to study the
Talmud."

Pinchus was torn between the joy of study and his anger that he could neither question the rebbe nor discuss with his fellow students, who memorized and moved on to the next page, day after day. He spoke of none of this with his parents, who indulged him in many ways, his father showering him with gifts and his mother with food.

His greatest pleasure was to hang around the central marketplace, where he could hear free form debate on virtually any topic of the day from why the chickens were not laying so many eggs this season to what political change across Europe might mean for the Jews. It was here that he discovered the joys of reading a newspaper. This was a large market town, not some little village, and it was a center of railroading for this region, thus a center for trade, and the marketplace attracted buyers and sellers from around the region. He could hear the music of Jewish Europe, itinerant musicians of every kind, all playing for the hope of a few coins and perhaps an engagement to entertain at a wedding.

In the marketplace, he was first introduced to the

world of books outside the Hebrew texts of the cheder. Pinchus stood that day by the herb seller's stall listening to talk about the herb seller's experiences when he was drafted into the army during the First World War. Pinchus tried to place this event in time but had no framework for doing so, and he tried to ask the herb seller and his friend, the man who sharpened knives, about when this event occurred and how long after the destruction of the Temple it might have been, and many other questions which occurred to him faster than he could get them out of his mouth. The two men showed no interest in the curiosity of the boy. They tolerated his presence but kept on with their discussion. Had a man in a dark suit not approached the knife sharpener, that would have ended Pinchus' education on this particular topic then and there. The man in the suit carried a physician's bag in one hand and a book in the other. "Here," he said to the boy. "Please hold this for me while I take out my knives," handing Pinchus the book. While he took the scalpels and knives from his bag and discussed with the knife man his precise instructions for the treatment of each instrument and the time he would need their return, Pinchus rubbed his hands over the book's cover and tried to decipher its title. The book fascinated him, its cover soft and enticing, the title intriguing at the same time that it was incomprehensible, in a language he did not recognize, and he touched it again and again as though his fingers might take some message from it that his eyes could not.

"Ah," said the physician as he finished his transaction "first, of all, it ended within your lifetime," then, watching the boy's hands, "You are interested in this book?"

"Yes," Pinchus answered, but I don't know what language this is. I read Hebrew, and I can speak Yiddish and German and Polish and Russian, some anyway, but I cannot make out what this is."

"You speak all those languages?"

"Well," Pinchus looked at the ground, "some better than others, sir."

"Come," said the Physician. "Walk along with me,

as I must see a patient, and I'll tell you about a great Polish author, who wrote in English and is the one of the greatest writers in all of literature. Thus began Pinchus education in the world outside the cheder. Any little gifts of money his father gave him added more books to the stacks in his room. The physician seemed amused with this pudgy little Jewish lad with a curiosity great enough for a university scholar. He made a deal with the boy. "Teach me some Yiddish so that I may attract some Jewish patients, and I will let you keep the books you find the most important."

So each taught and each learned, and the walls of Pinchus room grew thicker and more insulated with books. Some he had read five and six times over. He and the physician began to use English as the language for their discussions of whatever Pinchus happened to be reading at the moment, often three or four books at the same time.

Private Meijer, Max M.

July 27, 1944, somewhere in Northern France.
When they were pinned down by the Germans, they
learned all the nearby place names. When they
were on the move, pushing the Germans back faster
and faster, there was no time to bother with names.
They were just "somewhere in Northern France."
Journalists picked this up and submitted their stories
from "somewhere" because they thought it sounded
important, as though their location was such a
strategic secret that they were not permitted to name
it. To the troops it just meant another day of
moving on, leaning on the Germans, another day of
killing and trying not to be killed, another day of K-
rations, another day of smoking the Camels that
came along with the "K's", another day of watching
your own go down, sometimes wounded, sometimes
dead, always in the same place, "Somewhere".

Not very far behind them a clerk in the HQ tent
entered a note on headquarters "actions" list:

"Private Meijer, Max M. 4th Glider Squadron, 82nd Airborne division, Silver Star for gallantry in face of the enemy, promotion to corporal, effective immediately." The clerk had no idea whether Private Meijer were dead or alive, wounded or whole, on foot or in a truck, captured or still fighting. He was for the clerk just another entry on the "actions" list.

Eventually there came a moment when they stopped again. The weather was awful, the Germans stopped backpedaling, the 82nd learned the name of yet another town. They were bogged down somewhere near Andrassy. Max could feel exhaustion in every part of his body, but he was OK. Life took on a kind of normalcy. There was hot food from a field kitchen. Some old mail was delivered. Normally, people let you sleep. It might be your only real chance for a long time. The mail clerk would just lay the mail in your helmet if you were sleeping, but when he got to Meijer, Max, he tapped Max's boot. "Hey, Meijer. You better wake up for this one."

It took a while and a massive effort, but Max finally brought himself to a vague and rather foggy consciousness. No part of his body seemed to work right, and what did work hurt. Eventually he found the official envelope from battalion in his helmet. A medal, the letter said. He wondered what the hell for. He didn't have a lot of energy to devote to being thrilled or whatever it was he was supposed to be. He was more delighted to be alive to read the list than with the actual award and a promotion from private. "Big deal" thought Max. He couldn't know then that General Eisenhower himself would one day pin this medal on his chest, nor could he have worked up a lot of enthusiasm if he had. He couldn't know that his life had already changed. The change just hadn't caught up to him. Like all change, it would seem in retrospect to have been predictable. There was, of course, nothing predictable about it.

It was Eisenhower's idea to send in the gliders, but it was Max's idea to be in one. Actually, it was his idea to enlist even before the question of whether he would be drafted had come up. To his parents' dismay, he did just that and to their even greater dismay requested airborne school when he finished basic near the top of his class. Years later, when someone would ask why he had volunteered for airborne school, he would quote a line he remembered from a movie "Well" he would say. "It must have seemed like a good idea at the time." If you actually made it through airborne training and into the 82^{nd,} it was understood that you would volunteer, always, and for any mission. It was especially understood that the more dangerous the mission, the quicker you would be to volunteer. And, further, it was understood that if the mission was not only dangerous but absolutely crazy, at the very edge of madness, they didn't even have to ask for volunteers. You'd be there. So it was with the platoon in the flying wooden box.

Like all of the men of the 82nd, parachuting was beyond exciting for Max. It was hard to describe the sensation, something of a cross between a day at the office and the breath of life itself. With 60 some jumps behind him, there was a regularity to the jump, a rhythm he could enter the way Benny Goodman entered a song and then made it his own. He gloried in jumping. But being in a semi-flying, barely controllable plywood box, piloted by someone who had washed out of flight training was frightening. There were moments when he asked himself what a nice Jewish boy from Detroit was doing in this sinking box, praying along with 12 other men in "full combat gear" ("English translation: totally overloaded", they said) that no German machine gunner looked up, that no Stuka pilot looked down, that the box didn't fall out of the sky and kill them all from the sheer stupidity of its design. A box. That's all it was. The WACO CG-4a was an engineless wooden crate, high winged, the huge wings out of proportion to body, something a gang of overly active 11 year olds might have cobbled together in their back yards from scrap lumber. "I heard these was made by some coffin maker", said the gaunt faced soldier sitting next to him, Harkins, whose great granddaddy had died at the battle of Pea Ridge fighting against what was still called in his family "The War of Northern Aggression", and who had informed Max that he didn't much like Yankees but that he was calling a truce in that war until this one was over. "When we're done with these here Krauts, you watch out for me, Yankee-boy. We still got unfinished business." Harkins did not appear to be joking. Max took Harkins at his word but rather liked being thought of and disliked as a Yankee. He wondered if Harkins knew what a Jew was but didn't even consider trying to explain to Harkins the little irony which amused him so.

WACO stood for the Wichita Aircraft Corporation and was pronounced at the Wichita Aircraft Corporation as "Woccko." To the men of the 4th Glider Detachment, 82nd Airborne, it was the Whacko, and they all agreed that they were whacko even to think about being in one. Two gliders were towed aloft by a single transport plane, then cut loose over enemy territory to make their semi-controlled, but utterly silent, plummet to earth. For this flight of 5 C-45's and their 10 gliders it was five hours before light would break on D-Day, five hours before the Germans would know what was happening on the Normandy beaches where Hell would open its gates wider than anyone had ever imagined.

The sweat smell filled the glider even though it was cool, cold actually at 8,000 feet. Every man except Sgt. Lester sat on his helmet. There was an unspoken belief that a helmet would provide protection against ground fire in this armorless chariot. Each held his M1-carbine so tight that his knuckles showed white. Max would look at the men around him, look from their hands to his own, force himself to loosen his grip, to breathe calmly, to think of something else, only to look back in a moment and see that his hands had tightened their grip again. Only Lester stood. Sgt. Lester did not look nervous. For the only time since they first saw him at Fort Bragg, he seemed to regard them as though they were something more than low level life forms sent to earth for no purpose than to annoy him, and as he walked between them, he touched each on the shoulder. To each he said "Be strong! We'll land just fine. After that it's up to you. Follow your training, and you'll do just fine. Do what you've been trained to do!"

Each responded as he had been taught: "Airborne!"

Szmul

When he arrives at the hospital in Warsaw from the
rail station, he finds that the situation is not good.
His mother, wearing a large, broad brimmed and
spectacularly feathered hat, a fox wrap, and jewelry
sufficient to attest to the wealth of her many
admirers, stalks about the corridor alternately
wringing her hands and throwing them toward the
white tile ceiling. "Why, why, why" she is chanting
to herself.

"And why not?" thinks Szmul, "he is old and fat,
and he smokes and drinks too much, and he doesn't
sleep enough because he is too busy chasing
women. It's a miracle he's lasted this long." But
he says nothing. She is reveling in her self-pity and
projecting it as though she were on stage. He sees it
as another harmless excuse for a performance she
needs to give, one of the hundreds, thousands
perhaps, he has seen and understood since he was

old enough to have a sense of the behavior of women who were not his mother.

It will take almost two and a half months for the old man to die. In that time, Szmul will play the role of the language challenged buffoon close to 130 times to keep the role alive for his father, as if the old man might live to take the stage again and, of course, to keep his mother from driving him crazy. So long as she is busy, she is not so bad, but when she has time on her hands she loses control. The daily tasks which might occupy the energy of someone else, organizing papers and bills, getting costumes ready for the cleaner, doing something about the state of her hotel room, which has been well beyond the capabilities of the maids for some time, are invisible to her. If she lives long enough, he has thought, she will be crushed under the weight of her stuff when it is no longer possible to find any corner in which to shove it.

Each day he reads the papers, as many as he can find. Wherever he goes, the bars, the cafes, the billiard parlors, the headlines are all that he hears people talking about. The Nazis have started their march against Czechoslovakia, and everyone in Warsaw hopes that they will not attack Poland. "The Polish army will stop them" is a cry he hears everywhere, at the newsstands, in the coffee houses, wherever people come together, and life goes on as it always has but with a vitality which is frightening.

By the time his father breathes his last words to Szmul "get out while you can", the possibility of getting out is a dream.

No Names

Szmul is one of the last out of the bunker on
Krochmalna Street, where the Jews of the Warsaw
Ghetto made their last big stand. He is one of the
few left alive, and he knows that there is no choice
but to abandon the city. How did he come from
playing his father's role on the stage to living in
rubble piled on top of the remains of the basement
of what once was one of the most elegant buildings
in Warsaw, at this, once an important intersection of
living streets? How indeed? When the Polish Army
had to admit defeat, the Nazis made them pile their
weapons in the square not so far from the theater.
The guns sat there, ignored at first, by the Germans
through their arrogance. Ignored by the people
passing, out of fear or because they had no idea
what to do with them. When Szmul snatched up a
revolver and a cartridge belt, he had no special plan
in mind, no sense of destiny, no clear idea of how
he might use the weapon. As is always true in life,
even a random act leads to consequences. Perhaps

all acts are random, and we only think otherwise. Who knows? Things happen. Some will be good, some will be bad, depending on how you see them at the time or in retrospect in the years to come, if you are so fortunate as to have years to come. In Szmul's case, the thing which happened was that he watched two German soldiers shove an old man to the ground, then as one lifted him by his beard, the other kicked at the old man's right knee, breaking it so that his leg bent forward. The snap was loud, like the crack of a whip. As the old man screamed in the fire of his pain, Szmul, not thinking of the consequences, not worried about a future he could no longer imagine, not aware of anything else around him, drew the pistol from the pocket of his long coat and fired into a lock of blond hair creeping down from under the helmet and over the forehead of the German holding the old man's beard. As the soldier fell to the ground, he turned the gun on the second soldier, and, aiming carefully shot him through the right knee. For a moment, the soldier, stood on his left leg and looked at Szmul, looked at the yellow star on his coat and tried to raise his hand to the holster on his belt, but he seemed to have lost all muscle control save for the leg which held him up.

"Here," said Szmul, smiling. "Let me help you," and he unsnapped the flap of the soldier's holster, took the automatic pistol, and for a moment inspected it, aimed it at the man's other knee, and pulled the trigger. Nothing happened. He wondered if Hemingway knew how to fire these, and in that thought, saw in his mind the days in the Loire, felt the pull of the slide that loaded the shotgun and thought "why not?" It took two tries to figure out where to pull, but on the second try, he felt the slide move, heard the click as it reached the end of its travel, and relaxed his grip. The slide moved forward on its own. He aimed at the other knee. The soldier's good leg began to fold, and he put his hands in front of it, trying to protect it. His voice seemed to come from some great cavern as he vomited the words "Nein. Nein."

Szmul pulled the trigger, this time, there was a

gratifying snap, not the ear shattering boom of the revolver, but a precise sound, clean and surgical. The bullet passed through both of the man's hands and into what had been his knee. Szmul felt quite pleased with himself but had no sense of what he might do now. He stood there until he began to hear voices and to focus on the scene around him. Before he could reorient himself, he felt himself grabbed from behind, two hands on each of his arms. He struggled, but whoever had grabbed him already had his feet dragging as they pulled him into an alley. He ripped himself away from the hard hands and snapped the German pistol up to the chest of the man on his right, his finger squeezing the trigger, the gun pointed at the man's heart, right through the yellow star on his coat. The man's eyes were very large and his face was twisted against the pain that would come.

Somehow, Szmul willed his finger to stop, to relinquish its grip on death, made his hand give back the man's life. His hand fell to his side, the gun silent. The three of them stood in silence for a long time, breathing very hard. Then the man he had almost killed said "We need you. We are fighting the Germans. We'll all die in the end, but at least we'll die fighting. Join us." He said it in one burst of words. Szmul was silent, still processing what had just happened. "We need you. You're a fighter, and you could teach us. We have a few guns but we don't know how to use them well." He ran out of breath or, perhaps, things to say. He looked into Szmul's eyes.

For the first time, Szmul began to focus on their faces. The one he almost killed wore an old cap, pulled down low over his forehead. His face was that of one no longer a boy, not yet a man. Not, unlike Szmul's face in many ways. The other was not much different, a little dirtier, a little more unkempt. Both faces showed cheekbones made prominent by constant hunger, eyes retreating into the skull, lips cracked.

Szmul's head began to nod, less a gesture of agreement than one indicating deep thought, a weighing of options. After what seemed a long time, he spoke: "I know where there are guns. Getting them will be dangerous, but we could get a few if we're lucky and the Germans haven't figured out that they need to post guards. They began to walk toward the other end of the alley as voices behind them grew loud. "You have names?" Szmul asked. "No," said the one who had lost his cap. "No, we have no names. Only the living have names."

If he is to live, he knows he must get away. To the East, away from Germany he thinks, looking for the sun for some guidance. He has fought alongside other Jews, men and women without names, and they fought the Nazis and the police to a standstill, until the Germans had brought in the heavy guns and blasted everything to rubble. He has stayed behind to comfort a boy whose legs were crushed when a mortar shell exploded above them and brought down bricks and stone through the scraps of wood they had used to shore up their bunker. He took off his friend's cap and put it on his own head, pulled it down low, brushed his hand across his comrade's forehead, and shot him, one shot, through the Star of David and into the heart. But it was good, he thought. In spite of all they had lost, it was good. There was nothing invincible about these soldiers. Oh, he thought, if we had only had enough guns and ammunition. If we had any kind of preparation. We could fight these people. He stood in the midst of complete destruction and looked about one last time. There is smoke and fire and the shattered remains of more than the buildings which used to stand here. His father, he thinks, must have died by now. His mother, who can know? He stands divided. Search for her, or try for escape? If there is a way for her to survive, he thinks, she will find it. She has always found a way. If there is none, then there is no point in adding his life to hers without a fight. He has no plan. He has no prospects. He has no one to help him. He starts to walk, taking with him the German handgun with which he has fought, all the ammunition he can stuff in his pockets, and any scrap of food he can find. He knows that he is too late to find sanctuary, no matter what path he chooses. And so he walks through the night without any sense of direction.

Pinchus

There is a tapping on the door so soft that one might have missed it if one had not been listening especially for that sound. Pinchus, the "godless Jew" by his own proclamation, the former believer in a rational world, taps back, six taps, one for each point of the star. It is their code. A note slides under the door. Pinchus unfolds and smooths the paper with the care of a lover unfolding a note from his beloved. He should be in a hurry, but he knows what the note will say. What else could it say? He smooths it one more time.

"Leave now", the note says. "They are in the next block. You have no more than a few minutes before they come for you." Beneath the message is the outline of a rose.

Pinchus eats the note, relishing the drama of the act. He saw that in a movie, and it thrilled him. He fastens the flap of his knapsack, hoists it to his back, reaches out to close the door to the little room, so packed with books that it is well insulated against the cold. Of all the books, he takes with him but one: *Civilization and its Discontents.*

Then he closes the door on all his books, Freud and Huxley and Draper and all the others, and to everything he has known of life to that moment.

Majda

Majda has been everywhere on the trains. She
boards each with the same cold sense of appraisal,
looking always for someone who could be useful.
They are always the same these trains. Always the
same. Airless, as though the Germans would just as
soon everyone suffocate and save them the trouble
of dealing with these dead later. There was never
enough light to see very well and no hope of seeing
the outside world, if, of course, there was an outside
world. There was only the seasickness motion, the
constant kidney pounding of the wheels, and the
stench of shit and fear. In the darkness many who
were now dead, or worse, not yet dead, had written
messages to others also dead or soon to be dead, or
worse, not yet dead. Why is Majda on this train or
any of these trains for that matter? She has never
been caught by the Nazis. She has, in fact, put on
her ragged shawl, bent her head deep within its
folds, hunched her shoulders, and shuffled into line
for each of the trains because it is what she was

asked to do: "find the likely ones" she was told "and recruit them, and teach them, and train the best, and find another train, and recruit some more. Some of them will survive long enough to help the cause. Even if it is only one, you will have succeeded" No one said "until they find you out". There was no reason to say that.

Zaylie is standing. She would like to sit down but there is no room. She is incapable of pushing and shoving. She has no real idea of where she is or what has happened. She has no memory of how she hid in the top of the stairwell, nor how a hand reached out to help her onto the trolley, nor how she was able to reach the edge of the city. Shock does that to a person. She is, of course, exhausted and soon will fall asleep as she stands and then will collapse among the inanimate. Then she will likely suffocate among the bodies, and it will all be over. When it happens, the collapse to the final resting place on the floor of the cattle car, Majda is somehow next to Zaylie, catches her, and holds her so that she does not fall. They are like that for a moment. Then the girl seems to gain some sense of the world around her. At first she tries to speak but no sounds come from her mouth. Then she is able to ask "Where are we?"

"Who knows," says Majda. "Somewhere. Maybe in Germany, maybe Poland. Anywhere. We might be anywhere. But it makes no difference, wherever it is, we always end up in the place of death."

Majda reaches into the folds of the many layers of her rags and brings forth bread and, even more precious, a bottle of water, and gives it to Zaylie. She shields the girl from the sight of the others lest they both be killed for the food. Majda croons to the girl and almost sings to her that they will probably send her to a whorehouse barracks. Does she know what is a whorehouse? No, she does not know. Does she know how she came to be here? No, she has no idea. She answers Majda's question the way a sleeping child answers her mother's questions late at night. The mouth moves, but the mind is not at home. Does she know about sex? She knows about babies, but how one goes about making one she does not have much of a picture even when awake. Of what soldiers do to young girls she has no idea. Majda begins her education. For two full days while the train waits on a siding for more strategically important trains to pass by, Majda starts the process of turning her newest pupil into something useful. By the time the engineer throws his sack full of hot potatoes into the cab, then climbs aboard and gives the order to fire the boilers, Zaylie is beginning to awaken from the dream that was her life in her father's house.

The Lightening Rod

Judd "Lightning Rod" Palmer received his nickname in 1917 in what was once a farmer's field in France. In 1917, the field was crisscrossed with trenches and Palmer was the youngest Second Lieutenant in the Fighting 69th, the New York Irishers, named for the immigrant Irishmen dragged into the war between the states, a fight that was not theirs , but it was a fight, so they fought with gallantry, and their name was carried proudly through the War between the States, then into the great war, this collection of New York Polacks and Kikes and Sheenies and Hunkies and Paddies and all the others, some from peoples so obscure they didn't even rate ugly nicknames. In the 69th they were all "Irish" and they wore the unit's history as though it were really their own. In the 69th, even a Jew could rise in the officer ranks behind his Irish mask. In the 69th, they were all Irish.

His orders had been to drive the Germans out of a

set of trenches the Germans had taken from the Americans a week before. It had rained for four days, a heavy, bone chilling rain that turned once fertile farmland into bottomless, boot-sucking muck. Germans and allies alike were hunkered down in their trenches, cold, wet, bored, and sick, but secure in the belief that there was no possibility of an enemy attack in this goo.

Against all advice from his leaders, Palmer decided otherwise. He led his men in a crawl that was just one level above swimming. Continuous, rolling Thunder covered the sloshing sounds they made. When, near the enemy lines, he stood up to signal his men to start their attack, a sudden, astonishing, bolt of lightning gave the appearance of forking right through him. "God damn" said his First Sergeant, "he's a God-damned Irish lightning rod".

The 69th took the trenches from the stunned Germans, and he would be "The Irish Lightning Rod" through the rest of an illustrious career.

Zaylie

They enter the camp near the town of Gechen in the
night, and, even though the lights on high wooden
posts are very bright, their light is so diffused by the
fog that, in spite of brightness and glare, there is
little real illumination. Zaylie is oblivious to the
world around her, a city ringed in barbed wire, the
barbed wire ringed in electrified barbed wire. This
outer ring is mounted on posts taller than two men,
one standing shakily on the shoulders of another.
Each post is curved at the top, the curve pointing
back into the center of the camp, so that if someone
got that far, and wrapped his hands in rags against
the shock of the electricity, he would have try to get
over the top by hanging inverted as though
preparing for a back dive from a springboard and
then pulling himself from that position on top of the
curve of barbed wire turning his body while the
barbs ate at his flesh and the fire of the electrical
charge ran from wound to wound.
Once in a while, someone braved all that for a

chance at the outside world. It was considered sport among the guards who manned the watchtowers to wait until a prisoner had made the turn and might have tried to shove loose for the long drop to the ground before they began to shoot. Zaylie did not see them through the fog, any more than she saw any of what she passed by. First there was the Iron Eagle gate, with its Nazi eagle spread above a beautifully designed brick gate. It had been designed, like much of the camp by Speer, one of the finest architectural firms in Europe. Next came the beautifully wrought iron gate with the message *Kamp Gechen-A* on top and *Enter the New World* arching gracefully beneath. Then came the reception center, a building that might have been a field house for some vast athletic competition or perhaps the great central station for rail lines taking vacationers to every part of Europe. It was packed full of people, desperate people. Had Majda not been there to steer her through all of this, she would likely have stumbled and fallen, and who could imagine what would have happened to her.

One might ask what such a child must have thought of at such a time, but an answer to such a question would simply indicate that the questioner had no capacity for understanding. There is no thought in Zaylie's mind; there is barely anything that might be called a mind. Primitive ganglia respond to Majda's commands and move legs and arms through the mass of people and the maze of induction.

"We must remove our clothes now," says Majda, and when Zaylie stands motionless, uncomprehending, Majda says "Undress now!" And Zaylie begins to remove her clothes, the new Passover dress, the pretty black shoes with silver buckles. And she stands among a thousand others, naked and stunned. There is a steady stream of Kapos passing by, touching, probing, pinching. As the word spreads, even a few SS add themselves to the stream of touchers and probers, and there is more than one remark that this one may be too good for the Kapos' prostitution barracks. This one might be passed around among the corporals and the sergeants. "Why waste such a pretty thing on Jews, who won't live past their usefulness to us, anyway," asks an SS officer who has come to see what all the fuss is about.

When she is allowed to put on the gray uniform of the female prisoners, she is led off to a wooden barracks, packed with crudely built bunks, each filled with straw which is never changed, rank with the sweat and blood and all the possible bodily fluids of the dead and dying who have slept here before her.

Mina

Zaylie wept. She was alone, and she was very afraid. It was the stuff of nightmares, but she was pretty sure that it was no nightmare even as she hoped that it might be. She was perched on the edge of a crude bunk bed. The layer of coarse straw covering the wood stank, a wretched reminder that this was no dream. As she sobbed, she felt hands holding her and recoiled to the back of the bunk.

"It's all right," said a woman's voice. She would come to recognize the voice as Mina's, a voice still strong in a once strong body. "Well, it's not all right, but there's no point in spending your strength in tears. Spend it in joining us."

The words meant little to her, but the voice compelled some attention. She struggled to control the sobs and the shaking that went with them. She felt a cloth pressed into her hand, and she wiped at her eyes. It was just a rag; one she might have

thrown to the ground in disgust in her former life.
But, now, in this life, it was a gift, and she wiped
again. Mina's face began to take shape. It was a
face stretched tight with hunger, the cheekbones
bulging, the eyes peering out as though from dark
tunnels, but Zaylie found kindness in it.

"Here," said Mina. "Eat this, and I will tell you how
you will help us." She gave the girl a good sized
crust of bread and half a potato. Zaylie wolfed them
down, tracked down every crumb, and licked her
filthy fingers when there was nothing left.

"Everything I tell you will be terrible," said Mina.
"But it is how it is. We live in the belief that we
will have revenge. We will survive. Not me. Maybe
not you. But we will fight back, and somewhere,
some of us will survive."

As she spoke, there were six taps at the wooden
door. Majda entered the barracks.

Zaylie's heart jumped and she gasped for breath.

From the camp, past the row of barbed wire, past

the electrified fence, past the guard towers, past the fields plowed often so that they would stay soft to slow the feet of any runner who might get past all the other barriers to slow motion and then to exhaustion, past all these are farms, a town, forests, a river, all so close that anyone can see they are filled with normal life. At times one can see the people of the village of Gechen close enough to shout at them, though no one does for fear of being led to the courtyard between barracks 10 and 11. No one who has been lead to the courtyard between barracks 10 and 11 has ever returned. There the walls have been reinforced with concrete and contoured so that bullets will not ricochet back to the rifle squad. An SS Major who had been a structural engineer before the war had many very careful calculations to create those shapes. He had been very pleased when the first tests had shown how accurate his calculations had been. If one looked from the farms or the town one might even see the firing squad at work between barracks 10 and 11. No one on the farms or in the town seems ever to look in the direction of the camp.

One morning, walking less like a marionette than she has since she came to the camp, Zaylie asks Majda "What are those places?" Majda knows that it is time to advance her training. She gives the girl a little hug. "They are in the land of the living," she says, "and you will return there one day."

Zaylie looks at the ground and says nothing.

"You have a job to do there and a job to do here, and it is time you started to learn."

Partisans

"We have knives, not enough to give a real fight to the guards even if we had a gun, too, but enough to protect the group who will blow up the ovens. Majda will teach you to use the knife. Majda is with a Polish partisan group and she knows how to use knives."

Mina's words left Zaylie puzzled. "My Majda? Majda from the train?"

"Yes, your Majda." Mina tells her.

"Why is she here? Was she caught? Did someone turn her in?"

Mina's face was tight. "One of the Poles turned her in. If you are a Jew, trust only other Jews, and don't trust all of them." Mina did not try to explain that it was Majda who turned herself in.

The knives were too precious and too well hidden to risk taking them out for anything but the moment of uprising. Majda taught with a stick. Besides, she said, it was better than a knife if they were caught.

It was just a stick. At meal time, when there were the fewest guards on duty, Majda taught the way of the knife. The British commandos who parachuted in behind German lines had found Polish resistance groups, and had taught the Poles, and among the Poles was Majda. Majda knew the way of the knife, concealment, surprise, speed, death. Wherever the commandos taught their lessons, they left behind their final demonstration, always the same: two German soldiers who had stopped to see if these filthy peasants might be Jews, their throats slit before they knew they had confronted an enemy. The Fairbairn fighting knives of the British commandos were always concealed backhand along the arm. The free hand fluttered for a moment drawing the victim's attention, the move of a Gypsy pick-pocket. The weight shifted startlingly fast at the hips, then the hips stopped, slinging the knife arm forward faster than the arm could move by itself. By the time the victim sensed the danger, his life was pouring from him. Concealment, surprise, speed, death.

"But the Poles turned you in," said Zaylie.

"No, no" said Majda, "not the Poles.   Just one. The rest were OK."

Night after night they went through the moves of a well-trained British soldier, the concealment of the blade, the distraction with the free hand. The shift of the weight through the hips. The sudden flash of the blade. The slash across the throat.

 How can this be, thought Zaylie. In another life, dimly remembered and quite unreal, she had played with her friends and with Muttkele and worried about how she would do in the year-end examinations. Now she moved with Majda again and again and again, the concealment of the blade, the flutter of the free hand. The shift of the weight through the hips. The sudden flash of the blade. The slash across the throat.

Majda told Mina that the girl would soon be the master, better than the teacher. She was proud of her work.

Zaylie had no sense that any of this had meaning

outside this moment. She and Majda were dancing. That was all. Dancing with Majda became her life. Everything else was a dream.

If training for the knife was unreal for her, training for firing a gun was beyond dream stuff. They had no gun and little hope for one. The women had made a "gun" for teaching from scrap and sticks. Each time it was used it was reassembled and then disassembled when the lesson was over. There was nothing for them to be caught with but scraps of junk. From this unlikely device, each had learned from Majda how to load and fire a Webley-Vickers .380, surplus of the First World War. Majda had a Webley-Vickers, courtesy of one of the commandos. It was the only token of professorial pride and love he had to give to Majda. "I won't need it," he said. "I have me blade." Majda wrapped the gun carefully and buried it in the woods, where she could find it when the day would come for its use.

The first time Zaylie pulled the "trigger" of the

bundle of sticks, she was stunned to have Majda knock her hands high in the air with a broom handle while Mina and Sofia screamed into her ears and punched her shoulders. Her wrists hurt, and she was angry that they would hit her. Majda explained about the kick of the handgun and noise of firing it. Zaylie picked up the "gun", and they did it again. This time there was less surprise, but the broom handle still hurt. They did this for weeks, every night after the counting and before the lights were turned out. By the end of her training, Zaylie could make her shot, control the recoil, and bring the "gun" back on target in one smooth motion. She no longer heard the noise nor felt the pain.

The last night Majda said "Zaylie, you are a weapon now. Remember the murderers of your family when the time comes to kill, but don't become emotional. You can do that later. The job when you kill one of them is to be cold, the way they are. She looked hard into Zaylie's eyes and kissed the girl.

Max

There were many miracles in Normandy that day.
Max thought that getting out of the glider alive and
not in the sights of some German machine gunner
was his own personal miracle. There were other
miracles he would only learn about, some not for
years. On the beaches, the landing craft, every one
of which came from the factory of an eccentric
Irishman in New Orleans, worked as they were
supposed to work. Miraculously, air cover appeared
through the awful weather. The weather had been
so truly horrible that the Germans thought no
invasion could possibly take place that week let
alone that day. General Rommel was certain
nothing could happen, and he had gone to Berlin for
his wife's birthday. And perhaps most important of
all, Hitler was looking the other way toward the Pas
de Calais. He had carefully studied the intelligence
reports again and again. They told him that George
Patton would land with the army Patton had
assembled opposite Pas de Calais. It was a huge

army, equipped by the greatest production machine in the history of the world and led by that machine's greatest fighting general. It was a tank force greater than the world had ever seen, a tank force to fulfill General DeGaulle's prophecy that the allies would send 20,000 tanks against Hitler. It was fleshed with Patton's seasoned fighters, a force to cast fear into the heart of evil. It was a miracle that his intelligence service was so brilliant. Even he marveled at their level of excellence. Of course, this formidable assemblage was a complete fiction, all on paper, the intelligence carefully planted, but neither Hitler nor his spies had any way of knowing that. Had someone dared to tell him the truth, he would have laughed it off. He knew the Americans weren't clever enough for such a deception. He knew only that Patton was their best and that they would send their best. He knew that he must be prepared for the moment Patton came to his trap. If he could destroy Patton, he knew that he could win everything.

Worse yet for the Germans, Hitler was asleep when

the invasion began. His staff knew better then to disturb him, for he didn't like to be awakened. The punishment for disturbing him was severe. Von Rundstedt, stationed with his Panzer divisions across from Pas de Calais waited for permission to move his tanks to the real invasion site. If they arrived in time, they could destroy the Allied force, but only the sleeping Hitler could give permission for the movement. Von Rundstedt waited.

For Max, the greatest miracle that day was that the glider landed safely. Perhaps crashed is a more accurate word than landed, since it did take out two or three trees and destroyed itself in the process. But who cared? They were on the ground, albeit in a field not much larger than the space needed for a picnic, and the Germans had no idea yet that they were there. That invisibility would not last long, but for that moment, it was, truly, one of the miracles of the day. By the end of the day, the miracles would be over and many brave men would die. By the end of the day, Max had become so violently angry at those deaths that he set out to destroy three German positions deeply dug in behind the hedgerows. They fired through small breaks in the hedgerows, killing his comrades. Until that moment, even through all the training, he had thought that killing was not in his nature. He had believed right up to the moment he saw Haskins go down, a chunk of meat. He learned that it was there, somewhere in his nature, the thing that could find its purpose in killing, the dragon which hid in the fiery caves of his brain. In his anger he destroyed so many of the Germans that Sgt. Lester said of him to their captain "A regular Sergeant York, Sir, a regular goddamned Sergeant Alvin Goddamn 82nd Airborne York, Sir." That brought him the promotion to corporal and the medal.

But it was saving the lives of seven German soldiers that brought his promotion to T-SGT. He was among the first of the paratroops to make it into St-mer-Elise to cut the German communications lines. He and several others from the 4th Glider Division surprised a platoon of Wehrmacht defending the main road to the village. Before the Germans could shoulder their long, unwieldy Mauser rifles, he told them in his bookish and rather formal college German that they could surrender or die, it made no difference to him. The Germans were stunned, and laid down their weapons.

Max had no idea that the reports of his fluency in German could or would travel so far that anyone but the seven krauts would care.

As matters would have it, General Palmer cared. General "Lightning Rod Palmer", New York Irisher, career US Army, and son of the great tenor of the New York Opera star Isaac Palmer, known also south of Houston Street as Cantor Itzhak Palmernic of Congregation B'nai Jakub, cared very much.

Kleiner

Privat Teichmann and his partner Privat Karl
Schmedt are angry about these things as they patrol
the woods one more time: Feld-vebel Rauschinger,
who has assigned them to this duty for the twelfth
day in a row, the High Command for sticking their
unit here, the god-damned Jews for always trying to
escape so that it is necessary to send out patrols to
hunt them down, Feld-vebel Rauschinger for failing
to promote either of them to Korporal, and Feld-
vebel Rauschinger again for giving them this stupid,
baby-faced recruit, Max Kleiner, to train.
Kleiner is the only one of their tormentors they can
reach, so it is Kleiner who has received all of their
attention for three days now. Today, they will
execute their plan. They will help Kleiner to climb
into a tree still so leafy that he will be able to see
virtually nothing and so tall that he will not be able
to climb down with the heavy sniper's rifle they
have requisitioned for him It has taken them two of
those days to find a tree still holding its leaves and

almost impossible to climb without assistance. They have spent another day and a night figuring out a rope mechanism for getting Kleiner as high in the tree as possible. When they have him as high in the tree as they can get him and have passed the rifle to him, Privat Teichman cups his hand by his mouth and yells "And for God's sake, do not, whatever else you do, drop that rifle. It's the Feld-vebel's personal rifle." At the same time, Schmedt pulls on the rope and brings it somersaulting to the ground. To Teichman he whispers "That ought to keep him up there until Christmas. Without the gun, he might be able to get down, but with it he will be up there until we come for him."

It is hard for each of them to restrain his laughter until they are out of Kleiner's hearing.

Zaylie

There is the knock at the door, very light, almost
delicate. Tap tap tap, tap tap tap. Zaylie counts the
six sounds then looks over her shoulder. No one.
They have left her alone to sweep the corporals'
barracks. She opens the door a crack and shoves a
shirt complete with collar insignia through the
slender space. A hand takes it away and disappears.
A voice whispers "Mit *zein gezint*" and is gone.
Zaylie closes the door, slowly, quietly. She returns
to the sweeping and begins her search for the next
garment. They need a coat and a hat, and they will
have one complete SS uniform. As she goes to each
bed, she looks over her shoulder, then opens the
locker. She would most like to find someone who
has an extra. So far no one has said anything about
the missing garments because she has only taken
them where more than one existed. And Zaylie has
been careful to never take from the same soldier
twice. But she sweats with fear every time she puts
her hand on a locker. It is the kind of sweat that

bathes the head, then the armpits, then the small of the back, and finally creeps between the legs. She hates the fear and the sweat, but she does not let either stop her, for she hates the Germans even more.

Every day she sweeps a different barracks. Every day, she is inspected when she finishes the barracks. Every day, she is carefully, very carefully, searched. Hands find their way all over her body. At first she sobbed as they probed and poked. For the first weeks she wept and wept, thinking of her family, her Muttke, her friends. The Germans laughed at her sobbing. Anything made her cry, but she learned to control herself. The other women said it was part of her training, and she learned not to cry, at the thoughts, at the memories, at the hands, probing pinching, at the soldiers who came to her in the night. She learned not to cry.

She never has anything but her broom. After she has passed the sergeant, the corporal, the private, and whoever else shoves his hands up her dress and over her tiny breasts this day, she hands the broom dutifully to the woman in charge of her group of five, Zoshie Rosenzweig. Zoshie reports faithfully to the sergeant every day "All present, nothing missing, Herr Sergeant." They all know that one day the Herr Sergeant will kill her for her troubles if she doesn't oblige him by starving to death first, and then one of them will be promoted to her position.

They whisper when the opportunity is there, and they plan for the day when they will kill the sergeant.

Szmul

Szmul walks by night, sleeps by day. He eats grass and leaves to stop the pain in his stomach. He suspects that they have no nutritional value because he is deeply aware of how weak his body has become, but they stop the pain for a while. He walks, slower and slower, but he keeps on walking until the moment when his legs stop. He cannot lift his feet and sinks to the forest floor. He is leaning against the trunk of a very old tree, dozing, and trying to remember what it was like to be clean. "Was I ever clean?" he wonders. He tries to remember Paris, but it is too difficult to think, and he begins to drift into a dream about his mother, chattering and scolding him harshly about something. Her scolding becomes more and more shrill until it awakens him. His eyes are open now, but the chattering continues and the scolding becomes harsher and more intense.

High in the branches above him, in the dark thickness of leaves which block even light from reaching the ground, a fat red squirrel, its tail puffed to full volume in anger, infuriated by the alien presence of Privat Max Kleiner, leaps at the soldier's face.

A Letter

November 1944

Dearest Marlena,

Things are difficult here. Although I don't mean to complain. I know that things are terrible for you and the boys. I hope this letter finds all three of you safe and in good health and in as good spirits as these times can support.

For a soldier to be a sort of policeman at best and little more than a pest exterminator at worst is very difficult. Even my men, most of whom are rather pitiful conscripts, know that they should be fighting as true soldiers fight, against a worthy enemy. But these are our orders and we do what we must do.

As I thought of you and our beautiful home in our beloved Dresden, a picture formed in my mind of the boys at play, and I could not help but remember the time I destroyed the wasps' nest in the tree the

boys liked to climb. It was necessary to remove
that threat to the well-being of my sons, and I was
glad to knock it down and to spray it with gasoline
and burn the dangerous creatures. I felt a sense of
joy at accomplishing a frightening task (I was afraid
that the wasps would chase me down and sting me
until I was paralyzed. Some brave soldier, no?) I
was pleased when I thought they were all dead, a
danger to our home completely removed.

But I was saddened and then angry when the wasps
which had been outside the nest returned, looking
for their nest, now just a smear of ashes. I was
shocked that there were so many and that they kept
coming back to the only home they knew. As each
arrived and searched in the proper place for its now
demolished nest, I chased after it with the garden
shovel, killing them one at a time, until I began to
apologize to these loyal creatures for the necessity
of their deaths.

I was touched by their loyalty to their former home
and to their colony. I know that I had no choice but

their destruction lest they begin to rebuild the colony, and so I finished the job. It took days to find the last one, but in the end I killed them all.

It was much like that when we were ordered to destroy a village of Jews last week. They are a threat to our German way of life, and they must be exterminated. I know that, but I was touched much as I was by the wasps. It was too small a place to bother sending the people off to a camp, and, also that, we needed to make an example because of some incidents we have had recently. Some of our men on patrol have been killed in a particularly gruesome manner that I will not describe to you. We set up two machine guns in the village center – you could hardly call it a square it was so pitiful— and killed them all, we thought, and disposed of the bodies.

Days later I received reports that some had escaped, apparently, and were returning to the charred remains of the village. I took personal command of a small patrol and eradicated the three I found, more bundles of rags than humans, no matter how inferior. I could not help but think of the wasps, though, and I had the three bodies mutilated and hung from trees along the road. I hope that these grotesques will warn away any other survivors. In the end it will not likely do them any good, but I felt that it was the right thing to do, a tribute to the spirit of the insects. Anyway, it made me feel better.

I look forward to the day when all this is over, and I can return to my loving family. My love to you and the boys. I miss you very much.

Hans

Zaylie

Each night when the Germans come, she hopes for a
young one. The young ones are in a hurry and pay
little attention to anything but her. "Ah," they say.
"You are a pretty little one. You still have some
meat on your bones." Each night while one plows
his way into her, like a farmer trying to break up the
soil, she watches for her moment. Each night she
steals something, usually a bullet, once a grenade,
anything. Each night when their breathing is fast
and they can't help themselves and, finally, their
eyes close, her fingers are at work, feeling
everywhere for something. They brag to their
friends later and say things like "The Jew-girl
couldn't keep her hands off me. I gave it to her
really good."
All the women say she is the best, and they call her
the little magpie, and they pet her as gently as their
rough hands will allow. Such is the love of mothers
for the only daughters they will ever have.

And the cans of powder from the bullets fill up,

slowly, but night by night they do fill up, are wrapped in rags, buried in the secret place. Grenades truly rare, and most prized, are buried with them to wait for the day.

Mina

"The girl will take the uniform," Mina says. There is silence. "She could make it to a partisan camp and bring back real explosives. We have next to nothing," says Mina. "We will blow up what we can and as many of the beasts as we can, and we will die for very little. Even if we escape and get outside the walls, we will die. We are too old and weak to run. The girl might still be able to run and to escape the patrols and to find the partisans," she says. "If we die to get her out of the camp, so what? We are going to die anyway. At least with her there is a chance that we will be revenged."

Mina cannot be any older than an older sister might be. The same for the others. Zaylie can see in her face, in the sores on her legs, in all their faces, in the blossoming bruises and the bleeding sores, that she is right. They are all too old. They are near the end of the life expectancy of a prisoner, sixty-six days. They will soon die of starvation. Zaylie is older now, too. Five days on the train, five more in the camp. Fifty-six days left, a lifetime in the Nazi calendar for the Jews in this camp. "We will give you our strength," says Mina. Zaylie doesn't comprehend until each puts her pitiful share of food in Zaylie's bowl. Slowly, painfully, she comes to realize what that will mean. "It is our strength," Mina says. "You must accept it." They all nod. "You must!" she repeats.

Zaylie nods. She is sad. She understands that she will soon lose all her friends. But she is glad, too. These older women have taken her in as one of them. They have trusted her. Their trust warms her heart. It surrounds her like the wool coat she had when she was 8. It was thick and wavy and the color of the camel in the book Father bought for her birthday. Just to think of it took away the chill of the November night. She can feel the pleasure of pulling it around her and pulling the belt tight. She thinks of it each night as she tries to sleep after the Germans have come, wrapping its dream warmth about her in the cold night of her bed.

Pinchus

He stands at the crossroads in front of the village.
The three bodies, looking like bundles of rags more
than anything suggestive of real men, swing
rhythmically on a gentle breeze. Their hands are
nailed to their heads. The hands of one cover his
ears, another his eyes, and the last his mouth. Szmul
stands and watches them for a long time. Who did
this, he wonders, and why. He cannot imagine an
answer and after a long time starts to turn away.
Something stops him: a sound, a hollow thump,
rhythmic and sad.
Szmul raises the Mauser, drops to one knee, presses
the butt against his shoulder, presses his eye to the
scope. Filling the scope as he makes his way
through the village's dead, empty, central road is a
young man, no older than Szmul, clearly no German
soldier. No German is that thin nor dressed in such
rags. He could join the three scarecrows twisting in
the wind, and who could tell the difference? He is
beating his chest and chanting something. Szmul

can almost feel how hard this fellow is pounding his chest and begins to make out the sing song words: "I told them", thump, "I told them", thump. It is like the recitation of sins on *Yom Kippur*.

It is clear to Szmul that the other does not see him, and so he sits against a tree waiting, the Mauser lowered across his legs. He watches as the young man approaches, a face which might have been full yet deeply angled when it was decently fed, now an illustration of geometric shapes, clothing ventilated with rips and tears and ready to disintegrate, something that was once a shoe on his right foot, bloody toes showing through the remains of a stocking on his left. Amazingly, his glasses, though bent so that they hang across his nose at a bizarre angle, appear to be unbroken. As the other comes closer, Szmul can see that this appearance is the result of a complete lack of lenses in the frames. Szmul realizes that the boy will walk past him, unseeing, thumping and chanting until he walks into the river or a German patrol, if he does not say something. "*Vous macht a Yid?*" he asks in a very soft voice. The other continues his sad march, one step, two, three, and then he stops and turns toward Szmul. He cocks his head like a bird inspecting something it does not recognize, slows the beating of his fist against his chest until his hand drops to his side. It takes him a long time to make new words come from his lips. "I told them," he says. "*Ir macht gornischt*." He pauses for a long time "*gornischt*", he says, "I made nothing, I did nothing." He steps forward, his head leaning well ahead of his body, scanning back and forth across Szmul, trying to focus. "You're a Jew?" he asks. "One of us?" he asks in astonishment. Szmul nods his head up and down, then unsure that the boy can see his gesture, says "yes, but you and I seem to be the sum total of "us".

"Not from here?" the mourner asks, scanning again, trying to see if there is some feature he recognizes. "No," says Szmul. "Not from here."

"May I sit down?"

"Please" says Szmul, "join me. You can see that I am on the ground?"

"Yes", Pinchus reaches for the "glasses" with both hands and adjusts them with great care. "You are vague and fuzzy, but I can make out your shape. What are you doing here?"

"Well, I'm resting. In a while I am going to go looking for a German."

Pinchus face changes from curiosity to fear to panic in rapid stages. "You're going to turn me in?" His voice is almost a shriek.

"No, no, no" says Szmul. I am going to look for a German to shoot. I have declared war on the pigs. Speaking of pigs, do you keep kosher?"

"No." He spoke the single word in a tone mixed with pride and regret, as though confessing through it all the articles of his lack of faith.

"Then here. Eat these sausages. They are a gift from the Nazi who also gave me my rifle."

Pinchus held out his hand and took the sausages, but he was looking in astonishment at Szmul. "You have a gun?"

Szmul lifted the long rifle from his lap and held it close in front of Pinchus' face. He told the story of how he had come to own the weapon, how the German, like Newton's apple had fallen from the tree. He thought about giving Pinchus the pistol, looked at the fellow's glasses, and thought better of it.

"Can a Jew operate one?" He reached out to touch the rifle, running his fingers gently over its cold surfaces like a blind man reaching out to touch the face of a stranger in order to read his features. "I had never seen a real gun until the Nazis came. I have never touched one before this moment. But how do you know how to make it work?"

"All Quiet on the Western Front," Szmul says. Pinchus face contorts in puzzlement.

"The film, 'All Quiet on the Western Front' and, of course 'La Grand Illusion' and, to tell the truth, every American cowboy movie I could see. I remembered from watching the films. Some I only saw five times, maybe six, but who's counting. It took me a few tries, but it's not so difficult to figure out how it works. And shooting is just like playing billiards."

He watches Pinchus, who is now chewing faster and faster. He looks puzzled without slowing as he stuffs the sausages in his mouth.

"No," says Szmul. "That's not true. I mean, I saw all those movies. I learned a lot from them, but actually someone taught me how to shoot."

"So, why not just tell me that?" Pinchus asks in between chewing and swallowing.

"Because if I told you who it was, you wouldn't believe me." "Try me." Pinchus says through a mouthful of sausage. "I now believe nothing and everything."

"All right," Szmul shrugs. "You do know what billiards is, don't you?"

"Mmm, yes, sort of." He mumbles through the meat and gristle.

"Well, it's the same. You form a solid base, you take careful aim, and slowly and steadily you make your shot. Of course this thing isn't a billiard cue, it explodes in your ear and crashes into your shoulder as though you were a boy in the schoolyard and some bully hit you. The first time I tried it, it knocked me into a backward summersault. I was lucky I didn't kill myself."

"Food" Pinchus says. "Where do you get this food?"

"You may thank the same German who gave me his rifle. He also contributed his bread and this meat. I left most of the bread for the squirrel. I thought I owed it to him, but I kept a little. Here, take it. We'll go shopping in a little while."

Pinchus head is swimming. He stammers trying to make sufficient sense of this babble to put a question into words.

Szmul holds up his hand to silence the stammering and tells how he sat unknowingly at the base of the tree with the German sniper high above him, and how the angry squirrel must have attacked the soldier, who panicked and fell from the tree, snapping his neck faster than Szmul could tell the story. He explained, too, that shopping meant hunting for and killing a German or two. They always had food and water and extra ammunition. He could survive for days on what he took from a dead two-man patrol.

When the boy finished, he fell asleep, instantly. In a half an hour or so, he awakened talking, talking and shaking: "I wrote pamphlets. I walked from house to house. Eight thousand Jews lived here. Eight thousand. That's maybe, what, two thousand houses? I stopped at every one, every house. I told them. Go to the east. There may be hope. Where the Russians are, there could be hope, but the Germans give no hope. Here there is nothing but death waiting for you. I told them. I listened to the radio. I heard what was happening. I read Einstein's "Under the Shadow of Death". I took his warning from door to door.

They said the Germans told them that they should gather their things together, just what they could carry and that they would be taken to a transfer camp not far from town. From there they would be given work assignments and taken to places where workers were needed. They were told that they could earn their freedom and a place in the new society if they worked hard. And they believed this!

I told them! I told them! They all told me I was wrong. These men swinging from the trees. I know those men. I told them. They told me I was wrong."

He began to shake. He bent from side to side and beat his chest in rhythm.

Lightning Rod

General Palmer sat in his tent near the front, somewhere in France, trying to plan simultaneously for the 82nd's movement into Germany and for the German counterattack he knew would have to come. As he moved his hand across the battle map, a soldier came to the open tent flap and stood at attention. After a while General Palmer noticed the shift in light and looked up from the map.

Max had never before been in the presence of a general, and he would always remember how ice cold his sweat felt as it rolled down his back. The flight in the glider had been more frightening but not much. What could he have done so wrong that he had been summoned before the general, this general especially, the legendary Irishman?

"At ease, son, come in." The general waved his hand in the direction of a camp stool. "Sit down. Give me just a minute more with this map, and I'll pay full attention to you."

The general's tone of voice said that Max was not, in fact, in trouble. Max tried to think of what could be the reason for his being here, in this tent with Old Lightening Rod, if not for some kind of reprimand, but he could imagine nothing to warrant his presence here.

"Son," the General turned toward him. "I understand that you speak German. Is that right?"

"Well, yes sir, I took it in college, but I read it better than I speak it." Max's voice quavered a little, and he struggled to control it. "Conversation wasn't really taught in my classes. We read a lot, and we wrote some. They taught us a lot of grammar." He was embarrassed that he had said that last part.

"That's all right, son. I understand that you speak it well enough when you have to." Max must have looked puzzled because the general showed him a picture of the seven German soldiers with Max herding them along the road to division HQ. Max was stunned. He had never even seen the photographer. "I see from your service records that you are Jewish. You wouldn't just happen to speak Yiddish, would you?"

Max stiffened, on guard. Had there been a list of unlikely questions, this is the one he would have voted as absolute, total, least likely. There had been some jokes about his being a Jew but nothing different from the jokes about the Iowan in the unit. None of it had been vicious. He had not seen real anti-Semitism in the Army, although he had prepared himself for it. "Yes, sir. A little. My grandparents spoke it when I was a boy." He spoke very cautiously.

"That's good said the general" with a twist of the lips that might have been a smile. "You don't happen to speak Polish, too, do you?"

"No, sir", said Max

"Well, that's all right, Captain. We'll get you some

basic phrases over the next two days, and then you'll ship out."

Max was so confused that he didn't know what to ask, or if he should ask anything. What came out of his mouth was this: "Begging the General's pardon, Sir, but I'm just a sergeant, Sir."
"Never 'just' a sergeant." Said the general. "The Army runs on Sergeants and would collapse without them. As an officer, you must never forget that." He shuffled some papers back and forth on the field desk until he found a small package, which he inspected carefully through his reading glasses, then tossed to Max. "You'll need these for your new assignment, Captain."
Max caught the package, and looked at the general, hoping for some direction or anything resembling an explanation.
"Go ahead. Put them on, Captain. You'll need them in your new assignment."
Max looked at the box puzzling over the silver captain's bars.

Zaylie

Zaylie has put some distance between herself and the camp, but she is tired, hungry, and lost. Mercifully, the pounding headache from the explosions that got her through the barbed wire fences is not so bad as it was. She knows that the river she is to follow cannot be far. It was so close to the camp but now she has lost it and is quite disoriented and cannot even find her way out of the woods. She knows that the soldiers cannot be far behind her and is driven by panic.

All the trees look the same. All the leaves on the ground look the same. She thinks of Hansel and Gretel but knows that if she had a few bread crumbs she would eat them, not waste them to mark her trail. So what would it matter. She would still be lost and still be just as hungry. She sits down by a large, old tree, and her head drops almost immediately and dreams of a gingerbread house with immense brick ovens, their iron doors glowing red.

Hunters

In November the woods provide cover, but it is different from the verdant and impenetrable cover of the summertime forest. The oaks hold their leaves at least until midwinter, a dull rust stage curtain in front of the skeletal sycamores and elms, most of which have lost their foliage, and with that the forest has lost much of its color. The fir trees stay green, but it is a green of darkness and age. Even the forest floor, so colorful with the fallen leaves only a few days ago, has begun to lose its reds and yellows. Dull brown. Dull gray. These are the colors of the forest in November. They have a kind of naked beauty best appreciated from a distance, as in a painting or a photograph, perhaps one hung on the wall of a fashionable gallery with a warm and welcoming fire in the fireplace, the kind of gallery to which one receives invitations and which greets the guests with a tray of champagne. Here, in the woods in November, there is no waiter, and there is no champagne.

The underbrush has died back, providing little cover for the creatures of the forest but making it easier for the hunters to walk, stroll almost. The hunters give little attention to thoughts of beauty or the pleasures of an autumnal scene on this crisp, cold day, although they don't really mind being out here. They carry their Mausers loosely, chatting easily with each other, for after all, they are the hunters. Who is there to harm them? And the best part is that they are as far from feld-webel Rauschinger as they are likely to get for a long time. They are out chasing after the escaped Jews, mostly women, their sergeant has told them. Tired hungry women. What harm can they cause? The soldiers agree that it is not worth the trouble to capture them, unless one of them turns out to be better looking and less starved than those they have already caught. Much of their daily routine in and around the camp is pretty boring, and a chance for a walk in the woods and the praise of the sergeant if they can kill a few of the escapees makes for an agreeable morning.

They'll bring him back a couple of ears and he'll mark up a couple of additional credits toward their leave times. This is good. Life is all right. "Better a little cold breath here than really freezing against the Russians," Privat Teichmann says, gesturing at the woods with his free hand. He returns it to his pocket, though, without wasting any time.

Privat Karl Schmedt, his partner, thinks he sees something at a distance in the woods ahead of him and shifts his grip on the Mauser, but after a moment or two they recognize the uniform and agree that it is someone from one of their own patrols. "That fool is out without a coat", he laughs. "He'll regret that when the sun goes down." It is only November and already the winter's cold is upon them.

"Wait a minute" says Teichman, squinting. "Look again. I'm not so sure…"

Schmedt lifts the Mauser again. "Yes," he says. "I see what you mean. I don't think that's a German soldier." He shades his eyes with a cupped hand. "I don't even think it's a man. This could be our ticket to an early furlough."

"Well, well, well, what have we here?" says
Teichmann to Schmedt. He is looking through his
binoculars, weaving his head back and forth, and
making little throat sounds, like those a man sitting
down and watching the arrival of a promising roast
surrounded by beautiful steaming vegetables might
make.
He hands to glasses Schmedt. "Here, you look and
tell me what you see."
Schmedt fiddles with the adjustment and exclaims
suddenly "Oh, my God. It's our ticket to a weekend
at home, and, you know, a rather tasty looking little
morsel to boot."
"I could shoot it now, or we could have a little fun
with it, then shoot it. Or drag it back maybe. Do
you know if we get more points bringing back a live
one?"
"A good question," says Teichmann. I don't
actually know, but what the hell, let's worry about
that after we have a little fun."

They start off at an enthusiastic pace, the promise of amusement adding a liveliness to their steps.

As he speaks there is the slightest of movements in a pile of leaves 300 meters to their left, in a wooded copse across rolling fields, enough, perhaps, to attract the attention of one of the hawks circling on the wind, looking for squirrels. No lesser eye would see it, especially at this distance. Between this fine woods, with its mix of oak and fir and the little copse so far away are the gentle rolling hills of what might have once been grazing land, covered now with dried brown bouquets of wildflowers and tall grasses. Certainly, the two soldiers, still chatting amiably, see nothing, hear nothing, and if they had would have thought only that the wind rustled a few leaves or that some small creature had burrowed out of the sight of the hawks. After all what is there for them to fear in the woods. Unarmed and starving Jews? Women yet? Please.

Szmul

Szmul is quiet, but his tone is fierce. "Hit the ground," he says. And when Pinchus stands, looking puzzled, he adds: "Now!" He reaches up and yanks Pinchus to the ground. "Lie still." His whisper is rough and coarse sounding. When Pinchus moves, just to shift his weight a little, as if to see better, he growls "Now! You can't see anyway."

They are in a small copse, alone so far as they can tell. Far in front of them, across the rolling fields of dormant grass and dead flowers is a large wood. There is a row of oaks, leaves brown and dry, forming something of a curtain in front of the woods. Beyond that are trees and shrubs which have lost their leaves and fir trees which never lose theirs. At this distance, even at this time of year it is almost impossible to see into the forest, but it is a quiet and windless day, and even at this distance Szmul thinks that he has heard something. He kicks some leaves over Pinchus, and motions for Pinchus to do the same for him. His hope is that it is just the cry of some small animal. His fear is that it is a large German patrol looking for escapees or, worse yet, for its lost comrades and their killers. What to do if it is a patrol? Run or stay? Die now, die later? He feels a sense of freedom, given that choice. Not that he hasn't always acted with the sense of choice, but this is different. In the midst of dirt and hunger and fatigue, this produces a kind of euphoria, a sense of well-being he would not try to describe to Pinchus, whom he thinks of as Pinchus the worrier. He does not move, knowing that the leaves have covered them well enough to hide them or that they have not. They are just different paths to a destination.

His eyes cannot penetrate the layer after layer of trees, but he braces the rifle on its bipod and begins searching his field of vision through the sniper scope. It is astonishing, as though the curtain has parted, and he would like to remark on this ability of the scope, but he knows that he must be silent.

At first he sees nothing but the spaces between the trees, then, moving the scope a fragment, sees nothing, moves it again, and there it is: a German uniform poking out from behind the trunk of a massive fir tree. Szmul very, very slowly and in almost total silence pulls the lever back, then pushes it forward ever so slowly to chamber a round, tightens his grip on the rifle and moves his right index finger to the trigger. As the figure emerges from behind the tree, Szmul wonders what German soldier would be out on patrol in such ill-fitting trousers, actually rolled up at the bottom. He focuses his rifle just where the soldier's head will emerge from behind the tree, and he lets his finger rest a little more heavily on the trigger, no real pressure yet, just a shift in nuance, a billiard player's arranging of his muscles before the first practice stroke. "Good God!" he says.

Pinchus, still a little dazed from hitting the ground, looks at him in a puzzlement so complete as to leave him almost without words, just the slight movement of his lips, turned down in surprise.

"You believe in a god?" he asks.

"That" breathes Szmul, "is no German." He twists the sight, precise adjustments back and forth seeking perfect clarity through the kaleidoscope of trees, thick and thin. "It is no soldier, either." Pinchus looks more puzzled. He is waiting for an answer.

"It is…I swear it is a girl".

"A girl?" asks Pinchus, puzzled. "Is she one of us?"

"I can't tell, even with this scope, but I can see that she's no Aryan blonde." He relaxes his pressure on the trigger and moves his eye away from the gun sight and shakes his head to clear his vision. "No, it can't be a girl." He returns to the gun sight, shifting it for a better look. In doing so, he sees them, two of them.

One points his rifle at her. The other points at the ground and moves toward her. Szmul can see that her head has been shaved, the hair now grown out to an inch or so. An escaped prisoner, he thinks. The Germans were hunting her, not us. It is a question in his mind.

Zaylie awakens to see them coming toward her.
They have their rifles pointed directly at her. Her
legs are weak, but she manages to stand. One of the
soldiers motions for the other to stand back a few
feet and points at his rifle. The second soldier nods
and keeps his weapon trained on Zaylie's
midsection.
Zaylie sees that even if she can kill the nearest
soldier, the other one will shoot her. She thinks
quickly. Be raped again and die or kill this animal
and die. For her there is no choice. She smiles at
the soldier and moves her left hand to the top button
on her shirt and steps toward him. He smiles and
steps toward her. She flutters her hand as though to
caress his face. He smiles again, utters a little
sound of animal pleasure. Her right hand flashes
across his throat, the knife slicing just as she has
been taught. She can hear the sharp crack of the
rifle and smiles, pleased that she has done what she
can do.

Szmul and Pinchus

From the pile of leaves, there is a flash, a single
flash, a tiny movement, a question. Where has the
second German gone? With the flash there is a
crack, like the sound of a dead limb breaking under
its own weight. Crack, a little movement, silence.
That's all. The sound crosses the grassland and the
dry remains of the wildflowers, and the forest
echoes for a moment, then falls silent again. That's
all, no shouting, no fanfare, no sounds nor sights of
battle. The two soldiers are dead. They have gone
from life to death in an instant briefer than the one it
takes to realize that one has heard something. The
broad leaves of the sycamores and the pine needles
cushion their falls. They don't cry out because they
have heard nothing, because the brains, dead before
the pain signals could reach them, felt no pain.
Their falls to the forest floor make no sound, the
thick pad of leaves welcoming new matter to the
forest floor. There is only the quiet autumn air, chill
and crisp.

After a long time, the leaves move. Still on the ground, presenting little for anyone to see, Szmul carefully moves the bolt of his fine German sniper's long barrel Mauser model 98k. With a delicate touch he removes the empty shell, smells it and puts it into his pocket. He brings the rifle up to his nose, breathes in the air of the chamber, then closes the bolt almost silently, chambering a new cartridge. "Why do you do that?" asks the other bulge in the pile of leaves.

"Oh, I don't want their patrols to know anything about us, where we've been, what we've done, anything at all. So I always put the spent cartridges in my pocket and then I bury then somewhere else."

"No, not that. Why do you smell the bullets and the gun?"

"Ah, Pinchus the Writer, maker of pamphlets, chieftain of the tribe of worriers. Why do I smell the empty chamber? You know" he says, "At first I didn't realize that I did that. It just happened. I love that smell. It is the beautiful perfume of vengeance. Once I thought that the perfume of a woman was the most beautiful, most sensual aroma in the world. I was young then, and lacked experience. Here, take a…"

He had started to roll to his side to offer the weapon to Pinchus, but he stopped and became motionless. He put his finger to his lips, and pointed to the woods. "There is still the other", he said, carefully rolling back to his belly, and drawing the scope to his eye. He focused on an area well past the two bodies, and at two and a half times what the human eye could see he saw again what had almost looked like another German soldier but was not.

"We must go find her," he said. "What could she be but one of us? Can't leave her there."

Zhtarko

Zhtarko's camp is well hidden, not far from the river, deep in the woods. Men with rifles and submachine guns are dug in around the camp. Lookouts are posted in the trees at some distance from the camp and signal back to the ring of guards with mirrors in the daytime, flashlights at night. They are well supplied with British ammunition and batteries, air dropped by free Polish aviators who escaped to England. Food is, in relative terms, plentiful. They buy from the locals with the gold that comes in the airdrops and is of no use to them otherwise. Along the way these denizens of the city have all become skillful trappers, foragers, thieves. Hunger is not a problem: tobacco is the problem. There is none. They have taken to chopping up leaves and wrapping the stuff in other leaves. They say that these "cigarettes" taste like dog shit and smell worse and that smoking them is like inhaling kerosene. The standing joke after such complaints are voiced is "but thank god, they are plentiful".

There are rumors that Zhtarko has real tobacco and that he covers its aroma by burning leaves outside his shelter when he smokes it. And if he did, who would challenge him?

Zhtarko Kalposky is a large man. He is a little taller than most, but that is not what makes him large. He is like two normal men standing next to each other. He has great bulk, like a bull's, and a temper not much better. Before the war, he was first a policeman, then a criminal. In Krakow it took a great deal to be thrown off the police force. Zhtarko managed it. They said he had gone too far when he snapped the neck of his own division commander for demanding a larger slice of Zhtarko's bribe money. Had Zhtarko the good taste and sense of discretion to snap the commander's neck of an evening and at some distance from the headquarters, in a questionable neighborhood, for example, he might well have been forgiven and remained on the force. No one particularly liked the commander, anyway. But to do this in the bright light of the day and in front of almost everyone on duty at that very moment was simply too much. Zhtarko took his dismissal philosophically, spent the rest of the morning drinking vodka, and, in the afternoon, joined the gang of Stanko Brovich as an enforcer. He was well known within the gang, having arrested and found compelling reason to release most of its members, some many times. By the end of his first summer in the gang, he had so impressed the others that when he enforced Stanko right into the river Fluv for a sadly unsuccessful swimming lesson none was surprised. When asked if anyone objected to his becoming leader, no one objected. Likewise, when the Germans approached the city, and he announced that they were no longer a gang but a noble group of Polish resistance fighters, no one objected. There were those who were a little surprised that he did not take up with the Germans. The subject came up in his presence only once. "I am a pig and a thief and a murderer, but compared to them I am such that the Pope will canonize me for my good and gentle deeds. Any of you who wish to join up with a people who are worse than I am, go now in safety but expect no mercy from us or from your new friends." Each of his men turned to look in the eyes of someone near him. No one looked into Zhtarko's eyes for fear that he would take it as a challenge. It was said, and believed, Zhtarko feared no man, although it was also said and also believed that he feared a woman. They said, and they believed, that the one person in all the world he so feared was his wife, and it was also said that he feared her with such a fear that it bordered on the Old Testament fear of God. It was said, albeit never in his presence, that even the whispered mention of her name brought the look of panic into his eyes and a prodigious band of salt sweat streaming down his forehead as though he had eaten a Hungarian pepper at one bite.

Each man gave that slight cocking of the head that makes unnecessary a gesture so large as the shrugging of the shoulders. None of the men rose to leave.

They took to the woods, these men of the city, and they thrived, Zhtarko best of all. He proved an able leader. They shot a few Germans, robbed a supply train, beat a collaborator, shared their plunder with the villagers. Soon they were recognized in the villages, and word traveled. A partisan from another group arrived and gave them advice. Not long after that contact, Russian supplies showed up, then the air drops from England, guns, ammunition, money, medical supplies. Information about targets. The money was of little use to them, so they gave it to peasants and villagers. In return they had food, and information, and the good will of the "fields in which they grew" as Zhtarko put it. He had grown rather poetic in his days as a partisan leader. He grew a beard, grizzled and shaggy.

"This," said Zhtarko to his men, "is better than the criminal life" Then he thought for a moment. "Well, maybe if there were some good looking women, it would be better than the criminal life." Everyone nodded or grunted in agreement. Perhaps Zhtarko thought in that moment of his wife, whom he had not seen in a long, long time. Then again, perhaps he did not think of her just as he had not thought of her even in days gone by when he knew where she was, at home of course, when he was a policeman. Ah, there were pretty women in his district, and who could think of his wife when one of them needed help from the police? Now, a few pretty women, that would improve things here. Otherwise, life was not bad all. Different from the life they had known? Yes. Bad? No.

Zaylie

 Zaylie is confused, disoriented. She is convinced
that the second German shot her and that she is
dead. She heard the shot. Yet…and yet…and yet
she is still standing, knife in her hand, where she
was when she struck the nearest soldier, now
lifeless at her feet, his blood pouring from his throat
and soaking into the ground. And the other? He lies
where he stood, but without much of a head. She is
still in a daze when two others come through the
woods, and she slips the knife back into position
and readies herself. A thought crosses her mind that
she would like to have a moment or two to savor
her victory over the soldier before she must defend
herself again. All that training worked just as Majda
had told her it would, and she was filled with a
sense of pride. But there is not time for that. She
must deal with the next two.

As the two approach, one asks "Are you hungry?"
in German. When there is no answer he asks again
in Polish, then in Yiddish, then in French, and

finally in English. She stands as still as the trees around her, but after a while her head begins to nod. Later she will explain that she understood the words in all the languages, they had all been spoken at her father's table, but the situation was to her incomprehensible. Pinchus held out a piece of dark, heavy bread he had taken from the last German Szmul had shot. She reached out very cautiously with her left hand, the right hidden at her back. She tore at the bread with her teeth without taking her eyes away from the two men.

"What are you?" she asks.

"*Lantzmen*" Szmul answers. Pinchus nods. "Are you very hungry?" Szmul asks. She nods her head. "Here," he says and begins to search the pockets and belt packs of the second body. "You search that one, he's your trophy." She kneels, cautiously, and begins to search the body, wary, afraid that it will leap to life.

"What happened to that one?" she asks, pointing.

"I shot him. I would have shot the other one also, but you seem to have taken care of that. Where did you learn to … to do that? It was his turn to point."

"In the camp," she says. "A partisan. She taught me."

Szmul exhales deeply. "She taught you well. If you are ever angry with me, please just tell me. I'll apologize instantly. I promise."

Zaylie nods, as though thinking over this offer.

"Sure," she says. "Sure. Just keep your hands off me." She looks at each.

Each one raises his hands in a gesture that says such a thought would never exist.

"Do you want to come with us?" Pinchus asks.

"Where are you going?"

Pinchus looks to Szmul, who replies: "We have no destination. We just roam the woods looking for soldiers to shoot."

"I can't join you," she says. "I have to find the camp of Zhtarko the Pole and get supplies, explosives, to go back and blow up the ovens at the camp.

"Ovens, what ovens?" asks Szmul.

She explains to them about the camp.

When she has finished, Szmul nods his head.
"We'll go with you. No, I'll go with you. I can't speak for my friend."

"I'll go," Pinchus said. "It's not as though I have a lot of other plans, and I can't see well enough to survive on my own." He hesitates. "If there were some way that I, too, could kill a German along the way, I would be very grateful."

Szmul is going through the Germans' bodies getting their food and water, two fine backpacks, four packs of ammunition for his rifle, and two very clean Luger pistols complete with ammunition

Szmul and Pinchus and Zaylie

And so they set off, up the river Fluv. Here and there it was frozen over enough for them to walk on the ice. They were painfully aware of the tracks they left in the inevitable patches of snow and did everything they could to walk where they would leave no marks. They even tried walking in each other's footprints to hide the fact that there were three of them. Szmul had seen it in a movie, but they found that it was very hard to do and very time consuming, so they gave it up in favor of walking around the dangerous places and doing their best to cover their tracks when they had no choice. They stopped from time to time so that one might sleep, one guard the sleeper, and the other could climb above the river's icy banks to scout for danger. For days, they made decent progress, and the scouting trips found nothing. Then on her third trip into the night, Zaylie saw in the faint light of a slender moon what seemed at first to be a miniature house in a small clearing by deep woods. Without saying anything or looking around, she started toward what she had seen, slowly, silently.

When she had gone, Pinchus unfolded himself and got up from the ground, grunting and stretching like an old man. He stumbled toward the place where Szmul sat, his legs not yet fully awake. "Where is she going?", he asked.

It was too dark to see Szmul's face well even if he had his glasses, but he pictured a look of sadness, a look of resignation on the face of his friend. Perhaps it was in the tone of voice. Perhaps it was in the night air.

"I don't know exactly", Szmul said. "She is looking for something, but I don't know what it is. I have not had her experiences."

"Do you understand women?" Pinchus asked.

"No one understands women." Szmul answered.

Pinchus could picture a gesture of the eyes, a small movement of the hands, even though the darkness cloaked even the hint of gesture.

"Have you known many… I mean have you ever

been with a woman, you know, been with…?"
Pinchus stumbles over the words.

"A woman? Yes, actually…" He hesitated over the
word "many". "Yes, actually several."

There is a long silence, then Pinchus asked: "What,
what was it like? I mean…"

"To be with a woman? Well, the first time was a
little odd. I had no real idea of how anything
worked or where things went. The girl was not
much older than I, maybe she was even younger. I
don't know, but she seemed to know what to do. It
was during a performance. She was with the
acrobats and had hurt her ankle, so she couldn't go
on stage with them. While they were tossing each
other all over in front of the scenery, she was
initiating me into the rites of manhood behind the
scenery. We were pretty noisy, but the acrobats
shouted every time they performed a trick, and
nobody seemed to notice all the sounds we made.
Szmul fell silent, and his pause was so long that
Pinchus thought he might have fallen asleep, but
after a while he spoke again. As he spoke, the

clouds began to thin, and the first star appeared, a bright light in such a dark sky. "What it's like is to be bathed in warmth, both the warmth of the body and the warmth of the spirit. It is the opposite of tonight, alone and in the dark. It can be passionate or funny or even, sometimes, angry, but it is always filled with the warmth that women carry with them. They cannot help it, I think. It is part of their inheritance."

Pinchus thought for a long time until Szmul wondered if he perhaps had fallen asleep.

"I would like to have such an experience before I die," Pinchus said. Another star flickered into being among the clouds. As the sky cleared, it seemed to be getting colder, although either would have said but a few minutes before that it could not get much colder.

"Do you think we have long before we die?" Pinchus asked, as in other times he might have asked if a companion thought there would be time for coffee and strudel, a little talk about a bit of news.

"No," Szmul answered. "Not long."

Pinchus thought for a long time. "Do you think it would be all right if I asked Zaylie? She is the only woman I expect to see before some German gets lucky and finds us. Do you think it would be all right?"

Szmul did not hesitate in his answer. "No, I don't think so. We should not think of her in that way. She is our friend. She is one of us."

Pinchus nodded in the dark. He lay down again and pretended to sleep until finally sleep came.

She carefully inches her way along the edge of the forest, staying in the dark, walking on damp leaves, which make no sound as she steps on them, avoiding the snowy patches. When she is close enough, the moonlight allows her to see that it is a tent, big enough for two. It can only be German, she thinks, and they must be out looking for us. Her first thought is to return to the river to warn the others and to move on quickly.

Something in her presses her forward, though, and

her skin begins to tingle with excitement. Her heart is beating very fast as she pulls her knife from its sheath and starts toward the tent in the clearing. Then something stops her. If there are two soldiers, one must be awake, watching, just as Szmul is awake now, while Pinchus sleeps. She slips back into the shadows of the forest, not moving much while her eyes shift back and forth. For a long time, she sees nothing but the trees at the far side of the clearing, and then there is something, the lightest of movements, perhaps. She waits, her eyes searching. This time she sees it clearly. It is the glow from a cigarette, quickly concealed, but for that instant quite clear. Now that she knows what she is looking for, she relaxes and waits, sliding quietly to one knee. She is in the darkness, well hidden from any eye that might look this way. Her own eyes adjust, and she watches and waits. Eventually she can make out the movements of the soldier as he carefully snuffs out the glowing end. Then there is nothing. No movement. No sound. After a long time, she can watch him as he takes off his helmet and leans back against the tree. She waits. Her leg cramps a bit, but she does not move. She waits and watches.

When she can stand the pain in her leg no longer, she elevates herself ever so slowly. Even if one were looking in her direction, he would see no flash of movement, only the darkness of the forest. It is a relief to stand. She puts her weight on the cramped leg, flexes the muscles again and again until the cramp relaxes. Only then does she start to move, keeping always behind the edge of the woods, always in the darkness.

She is almost behind him now, and she moves just near enough to the clearing to watch him. He moves his left leg, drawing it up as though to stand, then straightening it out again. "He has a cramp, too," she thinks. Then there is a little groan. "Ah," she thinks. "He is asleep."

The knife is in her hand, the darkened commando blade hidden along her arm. She moves toward the back of the tree where the soldier rests, rehearsing in her mind what she will do next. In her mind she can see the horrible mistake, and her body becomes frighteningly hot. She does not know how to attack from behind the man. She must move in front of him, where he will be able to see her if he is awake. In an instant she is coated in sweat. It is bitter cold, yet she feels none of it. She is sick with fear that she will drop the knife and that the noise will resonate through the clearing like the fall of a mighty tree. She tries to wipe the sweat from her eyes by rubbing her face against her shoulders. She grasps the knife so hard that it digs into her arm and she draws her own blood. She forces herself to stand in place until her heart slows and her body begins to calm itself.

Only when there is no more sweat stinging her eyes, she begins to move forward, cautious of where she steps, sometimes moving in such small increments that it seems as though there is no movement at all. The tingling in her skin has spread across her body, and it feels warm and exciting. She is in front of the soldier, and she stands for a moment captivated by the sensations in her body. He doesn't move.

Slowly, ever so slowly, she lets her body slide toward the ground, gently straddling the man, feeling his breath on her face. She murmurs something wordless. He smiles as though in a dream, and his eyes open a bit. Then they open wider. He starts to rise up, his eyes wide open now. And she strikes, the knife slicing across the soldier's throat. She covers his mouth with her hand to stifle any cry he might make, but there is no cry. She has never felt like this in her life. The cold sweat is gone, and she feels a warmth throughout her body that leaves her weak.

Time passes. Minutes? Hours? She cannot tell. When she can move again, she lifts herself off the dead body, and creeps, slowly, carefully toward the tent.

Back at the river, she slips in to her own camp and stands in front of Szmul. She lays a German issue sweater very gently on the ground and unwraps it revealing tinned food, candles, ammunition, a stub of a pencil and a few sheets of writing paper, and perhaps most precious of all, a pair of eyeglasses. Szmul, nods, gives her a thumbs up, and, saying nothing about the blood all over her face and her jacket, closes his eyes and is asleep, instantly. Pinchus tries to burrow deeper into the dirt and deeper into sleep at the rapping on his head. "It's time for you to be on guard," Zaylie says.

He has been dreaming of food, vast quantities of food on immense buffet tables. Bread. All kinds of beautiful white breads and gorgeous braided yellow egg breads dripping with golden sesame seeds. And eggs. Eggs. Who ever thought that eggs would be the stuff of dreams? The eggs are the pure white of the Shabbos tablecloth on his mother's table, the rituals and ceremonies he scorned as superstitious nonsense becoming the stuff of his dreams. The yolks, the yolks are the pure golden yellow of the little finch in the cage in the parlor. And herring. Herring with cream. Pickled herring. Herring in wine. Herring in vinegar. Herring with schmaltz. Schmaltz with schmaltz, as his father would have said.

"What the…", This time the tap, tap, tap on his head annoys him and rouses him into something no longer sleep but something not yet consciousness. He rubs his eyes and shakes his head, trying to make sense of the world around him. It is night. His breath comes in frost clouds. There are those who awaken instantly and those who awaken as though they are climbing painfully from the bottom of a deep and slippery chasm. Such a one is Pinchus the scholar. He realizes that he is holding his breath and makes the effort to breath. He pulls his fists away from his eyes and sees that it is still night, but the stars are very bright. His first thought is that they make it too light to move out on the road, and the thought is enough for him to remember where he is.

"Why did you wake me?" He has slept on the ground for so long now that he doesn't notice whether he is stiff and sore or not. Whatever the hurts, aches, cramps, it is normal and barely worth paying attention to. "Oh, god," he says in mock prayer. "I hurt, therefore I am."

"Here," she says. "Try these." She puts the glasses in his hand.

He puts them on with great care, then looks all around. "Oh, my!" he says when he looks at her. What happened? Are you all right? You are covered in blood."

"Oh," she says, looking at her sleeves, feeling her face. "Oh, I am aren't I? It's OK. It's not my blood. I'll wash it off with some snow. Does that mean you can see now?"

"It's much better," he says. "They're not perfect, but I can actually make out details in what would otherwise be vague shapes for me. And I can actually see some things at a distance, even in the

night. It's a miracle. How did you get them?"
"I went shopping," she said. "Are you really awake?
I'm exhausted." She is asleep before her head finds
a pillow of snow and ice, but finds the strength to
say "You must guard."

"Sleep," he says, rubbing again at his eyes. "I'll
watch."
"No," she pulls herself back from the comfort of
sleep and speaks firmly, with the conviction of an
old veteran. "We'll just all end up asleep, and
they'll find us, and they'll skin us for lamp shades
and leave the living bodies to hang in the trees for
the crows to eat. There are patrols out there. I could
hear some of them, they make so much noise.
You'd think they'd be better trained," she says.
"Talk to me until I know that you are really awake.
Just keep it soft, very soft. Maybe there will be
clouds in a while, and we'll be able to get out of
here. I'll only sleep for a little while, and we'll
leave before the sun comes up. Tell me a story."
Szmul sits across from them, his back against the

steep riverbank, his head on his chest, his breathing heavy and regular.

"A story?" he says. "You want a story? What would you like, a fairy tale, a bedtime story?"
He thinks that she is already asleep, but she mutters "a bedtime story, tell me…"
He knows that she is right. It would be so easy to lower his head and close his eyes.
He stands and walks about, watching his own breath, testing out his newfound vision on the trees towering over the river's bank. He is awake, but the dreams of food are still in his head. Audience or no, he starts talking.

"My story," he is quiet for a moment. "I'll tell you my story" he says, speaking to Zaylie's still form as though he thought that she was awake. It will be the basis for my first great novel.
"All right. I was born hungry into a well to do Jewish merchant family in a prosperous village. My father was a dealer in precious metals. In Warsaw

he would have been a small timer, but in their village he was very well off and an important man in the community. His objective was to make money. My mother was a dealer in foods. Her objective was to make me fat. Each of my parents was good at his job. My father made money and my mother made me fat. I grew up Pinchus the Fat Kid. Oh, how I wanted to be thin. I prayed for thin. I wanted friends. I wanted girls. I wanted thin. Then the Nazis came, and I got thin. Everyone got thin. This is how I know that if there is a God, he is nothing but a practical joker. I prayed for thin, and he gave us the Nazis, and we all became very, very thin. I prayed for a girlfriend and what I got was a scrawny Nazi killer who's even dirtier than I am and who doesn't know she's a girl."

Zaylie made no movement. If she heard him, she gave no indication.

Pinchus whispers "God, should you exist. I change my childhood prayer. I'm sorry I asked. I retract all previous prayers. Make me fat again and you can have back the Nazis." Than in a deep voice, speaking very slowly, he points to the sky above and says "Kill them all, I'll make you fat again." Zaylie is still. Only a vague animal hiss escapes her lips. Is she snoring, or is it what she has for laughter? Pinchus cannot tell.

"Was that a laugh?" Pinchus asks, surprised. "You know how to laugh?" He gets no answer.

After an hour, she is awake. Szmul also stands and stretches. Pinchus is walking about in a great circle talking to himself. She throws the sweater to Szmul. "Here, you need this the most. And I have breakfast for us. And I brought this gun, but I don't know what kind it is. It isn't like yours.
Szmul walks over to her and takes the gun. "Ah," he says, hefting the weapon to his shoulder and imagining the grouse exploding from the field in front of his imagination. "I know what this is. Hemingway taught me how to use these. It's a shotgun, but not the kind you hunt with. It is the

kind they used in the trenches in the first war. Did you bring shells for it?" Her puzzlement is so great that she has no idea what he has asked nor how to ask him to explain.

He pumps the shotgun until he has ejected six shells. "It's all right," he says. "We'll find more. Zaylie, you are a genius. What you have found is the perfect weapon for a blind man." As they start up river again, he explains how the shotgun scatters its load, destroying anything in front of it. "Here," he says, handing the weapon to Pinchus. If the target is close enough, all you need to do is point this in the general direction and fire. It will knock down anything in its path. Just be sure you are close, and don't point the damned thing at me." Pinchus nods and focuses on a nearby tree as he caresses the shotgun. He cannot focus perfectly, but he has a pretty good idea of what he is looking at and how far away it is. "Now", he says, "I am a warrior." Then he looks at Szmul, puzzled. "Did you say Hemingway? Earnest Hemingway? The writer?"

"I said you wouldn't believe me if I told you who."
Szmul smiled and shrugged.

They are in high spirits as they hike along the river's frozen bed, and there is talk and even occasional laughter. Zaylie has cleaned off as much of the blood as she could. After a while, Szmul asks Zaylie "So, what do you want to be after the war."

"Dead," she says.

"Of course," he says. "We all want to be dead. Your curse is that you aren't dead, so if you aren't dead, what do you want to be?"

She waits a long time before answering. "I want to be Molly Picon in *Yiddle Mit'n Fiddle*. I want to wander from one small Jewish village to another with my father, playing our violins together. We'll play on market day and all the happy villagers will come out in their finest clothes to listen to us."
"Ah," he says with a sad shrug.
"And you", she asks Szmul. "What do you want to

be? You know, second place, after dead."

He responds quickly. "I want to be Hopalong Cassidy." He pronounces it "*keh-sadie*". "Or Tom Mix. You know they say Tom Mix is a Jew. They are Americans and they have guns. Oh, God, if only we had had guns like the Americans." He wipes his sleeve across his eyes.

"If we had guns in Warsaw at the beginning, we could have driven them off, and think how many decent people would still be alive. They were such cowards when we had a few guns." He paused. He looked up at the sky. "Why," he asked "do Jews never have guns? If there is a god, and if he is so all-wise, couldn't he have mentioned to someone the wisdom of arming ourselves before all of our families were gone, all of our lives destroyed? Couldn't he have spoken to one of those praying idiots and mentioned that the Nazis were going to slaughter us?"

"Me?" Says Pinchus without being asked. "I want to be in the French Resistance."

"The what! The French Resistance? You're in this resistance."

"Some resistance, Polski brutes and a few wretched Jews. No, I want to be in a real resistance. In the French resistance they wear those great berets, and they smoke Gauloise or Gitanes hanging out of the corners of their mouths, and they drink wine from the bottle and kill German *chazerim* with their garrotes. And all their women are incredible." Szmul is shocked. This is Pinchus?

Random-ness

Until now Pinchus could barely remember what it was like to have paper and a pencil, but he could not live without writing, so he wrote in his head as though dictating to an imaginary stenographer. But now, to actually have paper, to be able to write, it was as though he had been given a new life. He wrote in a tiny script to make the greatest use possible of the paper.

"So who could have imagined either part?" He wrote and the corners of his lips moved down with his shoulders, a shrug so involuntary, so automatic even he was not aware of it. "That this was to be my calling was not apparent to either my mother or my father, may their souls rest in peace, if of course there is a soul and if of course they actually had them. Certainly it was not apparent to me. I thought that I was destined to be a scholar, a writer, a thinker. What a joke. The saddest thing of all is to have a mind good enough to know that it is not a brilliant mind.

And who could have imagined that I would lead a life at this level of absurdity, with a random stranger who saved my life and who owed his life and his precious sniper's rifle to a squirrel? Did the soldier really panic over a squirrel, really fall from a tree and break his stupid, ugly Nazi neck? Is this story unbelievable because it is absurd? Is it more absurd than the slaughter of an entire people or more absurd than the belief that we lived in civilization or more absurd than our faith that we were safe? What kind of insanity made us believe that we were safe? Szmul says that the idiot panicked at the sight of a killer squirrel, but who knows? Szmul will improve on a story, you know. I must take his word for the beauty of the telescope, for I cannot see through it any better even with my new glasses. My new glasses, wonderful in their randomness. In same ranges, I can see fairly well, in others, I am still in the fog. Better I think than in the fog all the time. Random. In the end it is all random, isn't it? Was the squirrel an act of God or an act of the god of luck, Random-ness? Was that the reality of the god Ra of Egypt. Was he really the god of the random, save that the Egyptians did not know how to spell? Given what the God of Israel has done for the Jews of late, I am inclined to assign this favor to Random-ness, to whom is given the task of making sure that the universe is always governed by unthinkably bizarre and improbable acts.

And that I, a godless Jew, should stumble out of the most pitiful of scenes, in despair born of failure beyond any description, in need of something to fill the sad hole where my beliefs about myself and my rational universe had been, crying and beating my breast like a mourner over my lost mission to save my people, desperate for some excuse to live. That I should virtually stumble over the man who would give me a new sense of mission and the woman who would find for me the tool of my new trade, my glorious shotgun, if this is not the work of the utterly random, then I am wrong: There is a God." He stopped in his thoughts to look over toward his companions then continued writing. "And he is the greatest anti-Semite of them all." He shrugged and said out loud "So, what else is new?"

Watching him in spite of herself, Zaylie thinks that if the Nazis should ever capture them and ask if they are Jews, no matter what Pinchus says, no matter what language he speaks, that shrug will announce better than any banner that he is a Jew. She worries that she is beginning to think like him, crazy, rambling, babbling thoughts.

The Major

Major Hans Berghoff has again assembled his officers and non-commissioned officers in the farmhouse. He does his best in spite of his need to at least retain the aura of correctness. It has been a long time since he has been the immaculate officer he was when the war began. He has, at least, bathed in recent times, and his uniform is in somewhat better shape than those his men wear. He wonders at times how he came to this sorry pass. Is it better to give thanks that he is not yet on the Russian front or to lament that he is little better than these sorry troops he commands? Would it be better if he had joined the party? An Army officer should not have to ask such questions, he thinks, and he tries to bring his mind back, to focus on the task in front of him.

He looks at his men. They are dirty and they look tired. Even at attention, they almost seem to be melting. This duty has destroyed them he thinks as he paces the front of the room. The air in the room is almost poisonous with the foul breath and the sour body smell of these men who have been on the hunt day and night. They travel now in threes. Only one may sleep at a time. There must be two on guard at all times. These have been the rules since yet two more of their cohort died gurgling in their own blood.

Major Berghoff paces back to the center of the room, turns his back, then turns toward them. His voice is calm and low at the beginning. "Well," he says. "Now we know the enemy."

The men shift their eyes back and forth toward those around them. Each, in turn, shakes his head. These movements are subtle. Still, Major Berghoff could notice them if he so desired. Apparently he does not desire.

"Oh, you soldiers of the Third Reich, you magnificent Aryan warriors." Now his voice begins an ascent in pitch and tone and volume that will become so painful to his audience that they will cringe at the sound as they recoil from the message. "You have allowed your brothers to die at the hands of a Jew girl and you – the words become hammers – and you can do nothing. You, the cream of the Fuehrer's army cannot stop her?" It takes a great deal of effort to avoid letting his face turn to a sneer at this last remark. If these dregs are the cream, then what must the rest be like.

He paces back and forth across the front of the farmhouse as though in deep thought, his hands joined behind his back, a professor in mid lecture contemplating some interesting problem.

"Lantvarch", he says, stopping his promenade. "Lantvarch, you are the one who saw the girl and reported?"

Privat Lantvarch takes one pace forward, suppresses a smile at the recognition he has received and strikes the best pose of attention he can muster.

"Good" says the major. "Feldvebl. Take Lantvarch over by the trees and shoot him. And the rest of you. The next one who sees the girl and does not kill her will think that what I have shown Lantvarch is great mercy."

Stand off

No one moves. It is like a tableau of tribal life in a wax museum, lifelike but frozen, figures stopped forever in time, preserved in ancient amber without ever seeming to be real. On one side of this large shed, once a peasant's pig and chicken barn – the stench is a guidebook to the history of its inhabitants from the years before the war – there were twelve men, eight with rifles, four with blunt crude looking Russian made machine guns pointed at the two men facing them: Szmul and Pinchus. Even at a glance one can see that the twelve are in much better shape than Szmul and Pinchus. Their faces are not pinched with hunger. In fact, they look well fed. They all have heavy coats and sturdy boots. Szmul wears a mix of garments, the jacket of his once fine gray gabardine suit over the German winter issue coat, the best he can do to make sure that no one mistakes him for a Nazi soldier and shoots him from a distance. His boots, another gift from a dead German, would not be so bad if they fit. He has stuffed them with letters taken from the pockets of this same coat. Pinchus looks worse, if that is possible. His cheeks are great valleys, and his squint gives his face a hellish look, frightened and frightening at the same time.

Pinchus has his shotgun pointed into the center of the line of twelve. Szmul says that with a group so close together, he might kill one and wound two more with his first shot. That at this distance Pinchus' vision is still a little vague, even with his new glasses. Pinchus has never mentioned this to Szmul. Since neither Szmul nor the Poles know this, the standoff is real. Szmul has the sniper's rifle pointed toward the line of men and the Luger automatic pistol from Krochmalna Street pointed at the curly black hair on the back of the huge head of Zhtarko Kalposky, who has Zaylie backed up against a table and his hand on his belt buckle. That they will die in the exchange is obvious to both Pinchus and Szmul, but Zaylie is their comrade, and they will not see her violated, certainly not by this pig.

Blood flows from Zhtarko's face. Had he not moved with incredible speed and with luck equally incredible, her knife would have cut across his throat, and there would be no scene. At least it would be a different scene. He had grabbed her almost as soon they entered the barn. "Brought me a nice young one, did you? A pretty Jew-girl." He chortled and pawed at her. "Somebody give these men food while I make use of this present they have brought me."

Zaylie said nothing, but her face was tight. Szmul and Pinchus were stunned, frozen in mid-step. Before they could shout or raise their weapons, the knife flashed. Somehow Zhtarko managed to twist away just enough that the blade missed his throat and sliced through his cheek, catching on the bone and stopping just short of his right eye. He grasped Zaylie's throat in a hand like an ape's and bent her backward. "First this" he screams at her grabbing at his crotch, "then a miserable death. You will pay for my blood."

Szmul looks toward Pinchus, then, very quickly,

back to the pistol's sights. Pinchus understands the look. "Sure", he says. "*Yentz de goyim* -- Fuck the goys. Let's die like men." Szmul is shocked by Pinchus language, not the word, but that Pinchus even knew the word, let alone that he would say it. They nodded to each other, a farewell without words.

Without letting the muzzle of the shotgun move, Pinchus the scholar racks a round into the chamber, the sound of the shotgun's pump action in that silent room so loud the Poles cringe. No one moves so much as an eyelid.

Then one of them lowers his machine gun to point at the floor. The others follow, their faces contorted. All look toward the door behind Szmul and Pinchus.

Neither Szmul nor Pinchus allows himself to turn to see the new danger. They cannot let go of what little control they have of the tableau in front of them even as they know that it is finished by whatever new scene is developing.

"This" says a cold voice from behind them "is how

you behave when I am gone. You rape babies just like a Nazi? It's not bad enough you cheat on me when I am gone but you have to brutalize a fighter I have trained?"

"Oh, God" says Zhtarko. "Majda."

He turns toward Majda, releasing Zaylie from his grip.

"Ah," says Majda, seeing his cheek. "Too bad she missed. You were lucky."

"Have you idiots fed these children?"

Heads shake.

"Well, feed them. And someone bandage my idiot husband."

The Camp

To: Palmerik, R., General, USA
From: Meijer, Max, Colonel, USAR

Subject: Report, pursuant to direct orders

Nothing I can say will describe what I found when
we liberated the camp. I will try, though, now while
it is fresh in my mind because I think I shall never
be able to speak of it again. I can only hope that the
memories will fade. I was, by the time we arrived,
riding with the 92nd Cavalry Mechanized Recco
squadron, a part of the 12th armored. I still had the
small detachment of airborne that had left France
with me. By now, I was wearing a colonel's birds,
promoted again so that I would be senior to almost
any Nazi officer who might choose to surrender to
me. I assume that this was by your orders. I have
no idea what my actual rank is at this point but take
some pleasure in the thought that if some very high-
ranking Nazi should surrender to me, he may be

doing so to a Jewish private, who will go through the formalities and then kill the son of a bitch. I have seen too much for gentlemanly behavior to take over.

I did have a small unit surrender as we approached the camp. It is fortunate that it occurred before I entered the camp instead of after. I have been told that such units were rushing to the west in the hopes of surrendering to the Americans lest they be caught by the Russians. It was a German major who spoke English fairly well. He kept on telling me that he had not been responsible for what went on in the camp, that his troops were assigned outside the camp and that he had never seen what went on inside. Many of his men had not yet returned from their regular patrols, he told us, and he also told us that he believed that they would not resist capture by the Americans. I did not yet fully understand how deeply they feared capture by the Russians or by the partisan groups in the area, some of which were little more than bandit gangs.

Entry to the camp was delayed by a firefight with

the camp guards. It took almost two hours to overcome the resistance, but the 12th Cav troops and my detachment of Airborne acted bravely and skillfully and with, I am very pleased to say, only minor injuries and not many of those. When it was clear that there would be no more interference, the 12th Cav captain asked if I wanted to take my troops in first.

I had been briefed that it would be bad, but I had no concept of what "bad" could mean. There was at best little sanitation, and the stench was incredible. I did not yet understand how much of it was not from human waste but from wasted humanity. There was a platform above a rock pile covered with lime. Men, women, and children were pushed off the platform so that they could be aware as their broken bodies slowly gave up the life within. I was shown the place between buildings 11 and 12 where the camp commander used prisoners for target practice. People told me that he could empty the magazine of a Luger never missing the target and never hitting a vital organ.

I was stunned by the physical condition of the prisoners, the mark of death on their faces, and equally stunned by their spirit. At first there was hysterical crying as they did not know who we were. Then they cried as the word spread that the Americans had come, and I can only tell the truth that I cried along with them. People appeared from behind almost every building. These walking skeletons, starved beyond all comprehension, many ravaged by TB and God knows what else came to touch my sleeve and to ask if the Nazis would return. They tried to give me things; with great care one man pulled the stitches from his prison uniform and offered me his filthy yellow star. He apologized, saying in German, then in English, that it was the only thing that he had to give me. I took it and pinned it to my uniform jacket and spoke to him in Yiddish. Within an hour the word had spread all over the camp that the "*Americaner Rebbe*" had arrived to free them. How I became ordained I do not know, but I wore the star for all the time I was in the camp so that people would know that I was one of them. Several of my men, not a Jew among them, did the same. Many of the survivors asked first that we try to notify their relatives outside of Nazi Europe that they were alive, then for books of prayer, Yiddish newspapers, any news of the outside world, finally for food. We had, of course, no books of prayer or papers, but fortunately we had made preparations to feed people, although we had no idea it could be so many, and food began to arrive not long after we entered the camp. I wrote home, and friends and relatives sent books and papers, which people devoured with greater passion than the c-rations we had for them.

Count Zhtarko

Given the way things started in Zhtarko's camp, given how close they were to death, some might be surprised by the next few days. For lives so disoriented, so without logic, though, there was nothing especially odd to them about the warmth and camaraderie that followed Majda's arrival. Extreme and sudden shifts in reality no longer had meaning for them. In another time and another place any of this would have been bizarre and disorienting, like a nightmare. Now, it was as though one passed through a series of galleries in a museum of art, and in each there were paintings from a different period or style. Zhtarko become rather fatherly and laughed about his wound. "Look," he said, "the girl has made me a nobleman with a dueling scar. When the war is over, I'll introduce myself as Count Zhtarko." He tapped the bandage with a huge forefinger and laughed. That he would have raped and killed her the day before was for Zhtarko part of a distant past, something of no significance. Life changed, he changed with it. If you had asked him about the incident, he might have thought about it for a moment made some gesture of indifference, not to the event but to the question and said something like "Things are different, now." And for him that would have been all there was to say about the matter.

That he would have raped and killed her the day before was for Zaylie just another room she had passed through. There was only one room that could hold real meaning for her now, the last room, the one where the ovens consumed the future. She knew that in the last room, she would come alive. All the other rooms, the ones she had passed through, the rooms where she had once lived with her parents, the room that was her time in school, the room that had been a cattle car, all the rooms at Gechen, they were dead, and she knew that the person who had been through them was dead. Only the one who could go back to Gechen was alive. With Majda and Zhtarko they plan how they will return to the prison camp, how to avoid the Nazi patrols, how to survive the cold, where best to place the explosives. No, Majda cannot join them. She and some of Zhtarko's men have yet another camp to deal with. Zhtarko and the rest of his men are to keep the Nazis from destroying key roads and bridges. The Russians will come from the East or the Americans from the West. Either way, it is their job to see that the Germans can find neither hope nor safety in slowing the advances of those who have come to judge them. The best the partisans can do is to clothe the three against the cold, give them some food and enough explosives to do the job, and wish them luck. When it is time for the three to leave, they leave. There are no ceremonies, no sentimental good-byes, no hugging, no tears. They just disappear into the night. Three figures made grotesque by their heavy clothing and their precious backpacks.

They stay low in the frozen riverbed hoping to avoid the patrols. They cannot move in the daytime for fear of being spotted. At first the nights are cloudy and dark, so they can make progress down the river. It is hard going, this walking on ice. As the river froze, the wind carved peaks and valleys, making every step an act of bravery and skill. Still, they fall a lot, and in the cold each fall hurts, the pain added to the pain of all the previous falls. They don't speak much when they are on the march. They pull each other up and keep on. The wind tortures them, and yet it seems as though it means to save them, too. It clears the river ice of snow even as it falls, erasing their footprints, leaving no mark that they have ever been here. And then one night, clouds drift away, and the gray cover is pulled from them. They sky is filled with the light of stars beyond counting, solid fields of light. There is no moon, but this is the white light of death. It might as well be a million Nazi spotlights working everywhere for the patrols which hunt them. They have no choice but to stop and wait for the weather to change. With the clear skies comes the worst cold they have yet experienced. It is so cold that even the trees seem to suffer, their frozen branches shattering and falling. They take branches from the fir trees, using them as blankets, huddling together to conserve the warmth of their bodies, hoping that the branches will serve to keep in their heat and to cover their presence. To have a fire is unthinkable. When they have the energy to talk, they speak about what will happen when they near the camp, how to avoid the searchlights and to avoid being seen by the soldiers in the camp's towers. Now they must pray for bad weather. Even Pinchus agrees to it.

"Yes," he says. "Pray for the worst weather I can imagine. I shall pray to the god of foul weather and random events to bless us with his curses."

Three nights later the air loses some of its chill and bright lights of millions of stars in the sky disappear behind damp clouds, almost black. In the distance there is a crackle of light and pounding sounds of the funeral drum.

"Lightning," Pinchus says.

"Maybe," says Szmul watching the distant flashes. "Maybe gunfire."

Zaylie shudders. "Let's get out of here," she says.

Staying low is their only hope for not being seen, but it means they will see very little but the river's frozen path and whatever is immediately in front of them until they reach the big bend marked on the map Majda has drawn for them, their sign to crawl up the slippery banks and move toward the camp, the riskiest part of their journey, the part where they can be seen by anyone who cares to look. The backpacks filled with explosives weigh them down, so it is slow going, moving along the icy, angled surfaces. Walking above the river would be much easier, but here on the hard ice formations, they leave almost no footprints. On the ground above the river, the snow reveals every heavy step. So they move forward on ice, progressing slowly against the weight of their packs.

Zaylie is filled with the exhaustion of march, the foul, burnt acid taste of fear in her mouth and throat, fear that the Germans are finding their footprints in spite of all their care, tracking them and waiting for them. Her foot catches on a ripple in the ice, and she stumbles and falls. Against the cold and the pain even Zaylie has learned to curse. Szmul reaches down, grabs her elbow and hauls her upright. She nods in recognition. She is too filled with the effort and the sense of finality to hunt for words to thank him. She wonders where the Germans are, behind them and catching up, ahead and waiting for them. It matters not. The Germans will find them, and they will die, or the Germans will not find them. They will succeed in blowing up the ovens, then they will die. It is so easy. Once one understands that there is no future, that the only possible outcome is death, everything becomes easy. The pack becomes a little lighter. The feet stumble a little less. After all the chances for death that she has missed, she knows that this is the one she seeks, the one that will bring peace and silence and a merciful death to all memory.

She can tell that they are moving close to their position because she can feel the bend in the river. She knows that she will soon be able to hear the babble of voices, none so close that she can make out what they are saying but loud enough to fill in her sense of direction and position. It won't be long, now. She is proud. She and Szmul have lived to come this far. Where is Pinchus she knows not. He thought he heard something, perhaps only the wind or an animal, perhaps a patrol tracking them. He said that when one's sight was compromised one's hearing became more sensitive.

"It's all right," he said. "With this shotgun, I could hold off an army. I'll wait a moment to see if anyone is tracking us. If there's no one, I'll catch up quickly. After all, how could you lose someone walking on a river?"

They have not seen him since. She misses him, or, at least, would like to miss him, but she has no energy for it. Those things are no longer important, only finishing what they set out to do is important. She has no strength left for thought or emotion, for anything but the mission. So long as they are not spotted as they come over the river's banks, they will fulfill it. She can feel it everywhere in her body. She thinks about their timing. It must be good, but that should not be hard. As soon as they see the arc lights, they can count off the seconds between their cycles. There will be enough time to get close to the barbed wire before the lights come around again. Whether they can cut through the barbed wire before they are spotted from the towers is, of course, a gamble, but what other choice is there. It is a question she asks herself again and again. The answer is the same each time. There is no choice. Lie exposed in the snow and cut the wires.

The river bends, and she drags herself up the bank, stopping short of the top. She waits for the lights to begin their sweep and for Pinchus to catch up to them. Far behind her there is shouting and gunfire, then silence. She is too cold and tired and numb to think about what this means or even to care. Szmul tells her to go on. He'll wait a bit. "No" he says. "I won't wait. I'm going back to look for him. He's my responsibility. You are too. If they are tracking me, they won't find you, and when I find him we'll catch up to you. Why did I leave him alone?" He shakes his head back and forth. "What a blind fool he is."

"Look," he says. "Take my pack. You can use it as a balancer. You'll have enough dynamite to blow up the ovens three times over. And keep Majda's pistol where you can reach it. I have to go, to get him. He won't be able to find us." She looks at him once and nods. If she had any energy left, she would argue with him, tell him that he must stay with her, but she has only enough for the next step, and then the next. He helps her to add this pack to her burden then turns away as she turns back toward the camp. She keeps on moving as best she can, the extra pack a curse and a comfort, the weight of it a constant and painful reminder that she must go on. The wind returns and makes the cold even more bitter, but she is oblivious to it now. There is nothing left but to go on to the end.

Max

 In the three nights since he led his men into the
camp, Max has not found sleep. He has had, if one
were to make a generous estimate, six, maybe seven
hours of searching for it. He has had little success.
In spite of the incredible amount of work, finding
sufficient food and medicine and blankets, finding
nurses and doctors and engineers, taking a shovel or
lending a hand with a stretcher or comforting some
weeping skeleton, the relief of sleep would not
come to him.

He shuffled around in his tent, pretending to
organize his things by kerosene lantern light, gave
up, put on his heavy khaki sweater, knitted by some
woman at home he will never meet. He told
himself that he would think of her every day for the
rest of his life as he buttoned his field jacket over
the sweater. He pulled his gloves on stiff fingers,
pushed aside the tent flaps, and walked out into the
clear, cold night air. There were people
everywhere. Most were wrapped in khaki blankets,

which have been arriving by the truckload. "General Palmer's influence", he thought. They cluster in groups, talking, trying to make sense of their new reality, or walking about in circles mumbling, or perhaps praying, the blankets serving as prayer shawls. The night air fills with the icy fog of their words. He looked across empty fields toward the village, where a few lights blinked. Earlier in the day he asked one of the tank commanders to knock down the barbed wire fences, and the tanker had tackled the job with enthusiasm. Now one could, should one choose, walk toward the riverbank or to the village. It surprised him a little that even the fairly healthy people of the camp stayed where they were, never far from each other, rather than inspecting the region of their new freedom. He walked toward the river, seeking a little distance from everything in the camp.

Then in the darkness of the perimeter, well past the range of the search lights, he thought he saw a figure coming from the river towards him. It was hard to imagine that Germans would try retake the camp without a large force, but he and his men were wary of stragglers. What this was, though, he could not tell. He took the field glasses from his belt pack with his left hand and drew his model 1911 .45 automatic with his right. It does not have great range, but a forty-five will knock down anything it hits, and its feel was a comfort for him. As the searchlight passed by, he began to make out the shape of a person, so heavily padded in mismatched clothing and blankets that he could not even make a guess about what kind of person he was seeing. It seemed to be humpbacked, although it walked normally, if somewhat slowly and with an intense forward lean. As the figure moved closer, he called out "who are you?"

The figure stopped. It was still too far for him to see any details. He pointed his flashlight in the direction of the river, but dropped it and dove for the earth as he saw the flash of gunfire. He punched up his walkie-talkie: "Hey", he shouted, as though that would make a difference, "This is parachute one. I repeat parachute one. Give me steady searchlights at about zero niner zero degrees on the river side of the camp. Light up as many as you can, and prepare to give me some covering fire." There is the characteristic click and Niagara Falls background sound of the walkie-talkie. "That's affirmative, Parachute one. We're lighting them up now. Do you want covering fire now? We have the Krauts' tower guns fixed on the area you have indicated."

"No, hold fire. I repeat, hold fire. I'll be damned if I know what this is. Try to acquire the target, though. Fire only on my command."

"Wilco," says the voice in the scratchy waterfall. "We have you covered."

The figure coming from the river stands transfixed, blinded by four of the most powerful arc-lights in the world.

"Don't move!" Max shouts. "What language?" he shouts again, first in English, then German, Polish, then Yiddish."

It takes a long time for her to respond. "Yiddish" she says. "Polish, German, a little English, not much." The snow muffles her voice so that Max has to make her repeat herself several times as he comes closer. That it is a girl is clear from the first moment he has heard her voice. That she speaks Yiddish tells him that she is not a Nazi. That she is bundled as she is tells him that she must be very cold. He zigzags his way toward her, moving to a different side each time he speaks, and staying low, just in case she starts to shoot at the sound of his voice. He can't imagine that she can see him with the spotlights in her eyes, but he takes no chances. When he is next to her, he takes the pistol from her hand. He recognizes its feel immediately, British Webley .380, and he tucks it in his belt. He punches the talk button and says "shut down the lights except for one. Keep it well ahead of us so we can see our way back. She blinks for a long time before her vision begins to return to normal. He holds her arm and guides her toward the camp. "Will you shoot me," she asks? "No," he says. "We're Americans, you know, the American Army."

She stops and looks at him as well as she can. "But you speak Yiddish", she says. Max puzzles over her bewilderment and takes a moment to realize how bizarre this must be to the girl. "Yes," he says. "I am a Jew in the American Army."

By the time the sappers have come and gone with her backpacks full of explosives, she has begun to feel the warmth of the US Government Issue kerosene stoves in what was the SS officers' quarters.

"I have failed," she said, head bent over a mug of hot broth. "I have failed."

Eisenhower

Before the medal ceremony began, Colonel Meijer and General Palmer sat together in the parlor of what must have been the home of a very prosperous family. There is a fire in the great stone fireplace. The chimney draws imperfectly, and there is a pleasantly smoky warmth throughout the room. The two men add to the thickness in the air as each smokes an Uppmann Presidente from General Palmer's treasured supply.

"I don't know what else to do, sir" says Max. "I've looked all over Europe. I've contacted every liberator I could track down. I've followed every lead you've given me. I've had people looking at every agency. We went to the place where her family lived. There was no one, not even anyone left to remember them."

Palmer nodded.

"I believe at this point that there is no living relative, no surviving prisoner who befriended her, no indication that the two men who saved her life and took on her mission survived their last encounter with the Germans. There may be some Polish partisans who would know her, but they have simply melted into the population. I believe at this point that she is alone in the world, with no place to go, and I believe that she cannot survive on her own. Sir, from the moment she fully understood that we had stopped the killing, she has never let me out of her sight. To get away today I had to leave her with two of my best men and to give her my solemn promise that I would return for her."

General Palmer shook his head and exhaled a heavy cloud from the Uppmann. "Are you sleeping with her?"

"No sir," Max shook his head.

"Why not?" the General asked.

"Well, sir, first of all I'm married and beside that she's not much more than a girl. It wouldn't be right, sir."

"You're a good man, Meijer, but what are you going to do with her?"

"I don't see what else I can do, sir. I'm planning on

taking her home with me."

General Palmer appeared to think about that for a moment. "Have you told your wife this?"

"Yes, sir. I wrote Mindy, but I wasn't completely honest. I said that I had found a relative who had no one else. I thought that might make it a little better. I believe that she'll understand, sir. I can't leave the girl here."

General Palmer flicked a speck of dust from his trousers. "No, no, you can't. And who is to say that she is not a relative of yours, or of mine for that matter?"

Max was puzzled by Palmer's last remark and would have asked about it. What he would have asked he was not sure, but instead something different came out of his mouth." I know that we can take care of her in the sense of food and shelter, but I don't know how to really help her. She seems pretty shell shocked to me. I don't know what to do about that."General Palmer seemed to think for a moment. "I may know someone who can help. Are you familiar with Dr. Carl Menninger's work? "

"Well, I remember something, a bit, from a psych course, but I thought his name was Will."

"Actually, that's his brother. Probably better known, but Carl has been working with the Army for quite some time, now. We have thousands coming home battle fatigued, shell shocked, crippled, some physically, some mentally, some both. Menninger is developing programs to help those men. When I had to brief Ike on your action, I told him about the girl. He was the one who suggested Menninger."

Max's mind was overwhelmed with questions, but, before he could formulate one, Eisenhower's dog robber, a Colonel wearing his aide-de camp's epaulets, came into the room. "General Eisenhower's ready for you now, gentlemen." Max struggled with the thought that it was not a lifetime ago, only time that could be measured in nothing more than months that he had spoken a few words of German and changed his life forever. But he shook that off, rose and stretched a little, stiff from sitting, and followed the Lightning Rod.

Dr. Carl

The windows in the office wing of the Naval Hospital in Washington, D.C. stopped just short of the high ceilings of the old building, magnifying the sunlight pouring through the glass, overwhelming the light from the ancient fixtures, and almost spotlighting the immaculate dress whites of the Navy Corpsman who greeted them. Max thought that Navy whites made his own uniform look rather drab by comparison. "Of course," he said, "that's why it's called olive drab".

"Sir?"

"I "actually said that out loud, didn't I. Probably a sign of early senility.   I was admiring your dress whites and sort of laughing at myself. It's a good looking uniform. I noticed your ribbons, too. You were in the Pacific?"

"Yes, Sir. I was with the First Marines."

Max started to say something, but, before the words came, Dr. Menninger came into the waiting room. He was a tall man, wearing a gray suit, a bright red tie hanging loose. "Michael," he said to the Corpsman. "Would you please go into my office and keep the young woman company while I speak with the Colonel? She'll be comfortable with you. Someday that boy will be one hell of a fine physician, but that's not what we're here to talk about." Meninnger gestured for Max to sit. "Forgive me for sounding as though I am rushing through this. I've really given it a lot of thought. She is both very different from the young soldiers and marines I see and, at the same time, very similar. I think she has problems beyond any I have ever seen, in terms of the sheer depth of her wounds. Although what I think is going on inside her, it seems to me possible that this young woman may never fully recover from what she has been through. People are resilient, and she may find a way to deal with her experiences in ways I cannot predict. People think I know so much, but in truth we know very little about this kind of damage and are just trying to learn how to deal with it." Max asked what he could do for Zaylie, and Menninger told him to keep her in situations in which she could feel safe, to let her heal in her own way and in her own time. "I am not sure," he said, "if it is better that she recovers her memories or keeps them buried forever because I cannot imagine what those memories must be like. All I can say is to let her take all the time she needs."

Marshall Fine

Over the years Zaylie produced more needlepoint
pieces than there were places to put them. From
time to time Max was able to persuade Zaylie to
allow him to have them framed and to donate them
the Jewish Elders' Residence. Should you walk the
halls of the building, just across from the JCC, you
would find an art gallery's worth of her work. No
one thought a lot about them. They were displayed
somewhat randomly in rooms and corridors, just
something donated, neither ignored nor celebrated.
Eventually, they all made their way to a small
classroom. Then one day, one of the residents,
Marshall Fine, wandered into that room looking for
the housekeeper and was stunned by what he saw.
They began to take a regular place in the thoughts
of Marshall Fine, who had turned his art gallery
over to his daughter and retired to this place to be
among his cronies for at least part of the year and,
"anyway", he said, he didn't like Florida because it
was full of "old people and cockroaches the size of

dachshunds, and it's too fucking hot". When people told him how wonderful Florida was, he would waggle a cigar at them and say "I was born in Detroit, I raised my family in Detroit, and, by God, I'm going to be buried right here in Detroit right next to Adele, so I might just as well have my cranky God damned old age here in Detroit instead of some fucking nest for mosquitoes, alligators, and dried up old ladies." That usually ended any further remarks on the merits of Florida. Every day he sat at lunch with his usual group augmented occasionally by the facility's manager, Marty Bensinger, who joined a different group each day. She was popular with the residents, the "newly–old" and the "get me my boots and my crutches—old" as they called themselves. And she was popular with those whose expenses had to be subsidized and with those who, like Fine, could, and often did, quietly, much of the subsidizing. She was popular for many reasons. She was young, and she was good looking, and many a resident tried to introduce her to an unmarried grandson. But mostly she was popular because she listened, and she paid real attention. When a resident had a complaint, Marty saw to it that it was looked into and, if at all possible, fixed. When a resident had a suggestion, Marty considered it carefully, discussed it with the other residents, and again, if it were possible, saw to it that the suggestion had a good trial.

And so it was that day at lunch that Marshall said: "You know, Marty, I've been looking at those needlepoint pieces in the small classroom. Now that the old lady has passed on, it might make sense to have them appraised. Unless you've already done something like that, of course.

Marty looked off into a corner of the room, dragged the corners of her mouth, nodded her head back and forth, raised an eyebrow and lowered it again, gave a delicate shrug and a faint wave of her left hand, looked back at Marshall. "No", she said. "I had never really even thought about it. They're covered under the general insurance policy on the building, but if they have value beyond the fact that they're nice, they should be under separate coverage. Can you assess their value, Marsh?"

"No," said Fine. "It isn't that I wouldn't. This just isn't my area, but you know Ruthie. She loves this kind of stuff, eats it up. Call her, or for that matter, I can suggest that she call you. It isn't as though I'm not picking her up for supper tonight."

"Thanks," said Marty. "But that's OK. I'll call her at the gallery right after lunch."

Ruth Fine

So it was that one beautifully snowy February afternoon Ruth Fine (BA Yale, MFA School of Visual Art) and Marty Bensinger strolled the hallways together. Ruth had a clipboard in hand and a pencil tucked behind her ear, but she had yet to make a note.

"This is breathtaking," she said. "I can't believe I've never seen all of these. You know, I always pick up dad or he picks me up, and I've just never walked the halls back here or even seen this room. I feel like the people who first saw Grandma Moses. They must have been stunned. Seeing this entire collection is utterly overwhelming. These pieces are quite astonishing. They are almost cute, with the childish figures and the pretty faces, even on the boys. But somehow they don't seem cute. I'm not quite sure what it is. And, what fine work to get so much detail and expression into those faces. Look at this one of the little girl sitting at the top of the stairs, and oh, this one of the two boys marching into the woods. This little fellow has a popgun over his shoulder and the other is carrying a book. It is as though they are going for a stroll, and one is playing at being a hunter while the other is going to find a good tree to lean against while he reads his favorite stories." Ruth begins to make notes, pausing in front of each piece, lingering in front of some to make quick sketches of the design. She is especially intrigued with one showing two boys and a girl. Are they meant to all be the same children, she wonders. They are strolling along a riverbank in the light of early morning, each wearing a backpack of the kind one associates with European school children. Over them a bright, yellow star shines. Ruth imagines that they are on their way to the country to have a picnic.

It takes the entire afternoon to complete her sketching and note taking, barely noticing when Marty is called back to her office to take a phone call.

Her pages filled with notes, she stops at Marty's office for her coat and winter boots. "Dad was right" she says to Marty. "These are definitely worth something, but I have to do some research to put a dollar figure to that. I'll call you in a couple of days and we can have lunch and talk about what I find out."

It is only as she walks through the snow to her car that a sense of sadness and loss consumes her and she leans against her car gasping for breath.

Passover

And then it was erev Pesach again, time for the
Seder to return to the Meijer's home. Who could
imagine that four years had gone by? So fast. So
fast. Each year the partners' wives came early to
offer whatever help they might give. So far, after
all, it was quite early, only Hal Bernstein's wife,
Elaine, was helping Sylvia to supervise the caterer's
people in the newly remodeled kitchen at the
Meijer's'. Since there was not a lot of turnover at
Katz Kosher Katering, Mr. Katz and virtually his
entire staff knew the house and the kitchen, in spite
of the remodeling. There was, in truth, very little
supervising to do except, of course, for reminding
Mr. Katz that the meal should be as Atkins friendly
this year as was humanly possible. Mr. Katz assured
the women that even the Matzahs had the Atkins
stamp, so Elaine and Sylvia were doing their best to
fuss a little without actually getting in the caterers'
way. From concerns about food, their conversation
had drifted through certain health concerns to

concerns about weight to going over changes since the last time it was the Meijers' turn to host the Seder. This was also part of the rather subconscious Passover ritual at each of the homes.

There was, of course, the topic of Barney Garber's new wife. That was new even since last year, let alone since four years ago, so it was a very hot topic. All the wives worried about losing out to a younger woman, but who would have thought that it would be Sandy who would be the first to go? She was, at fifty, the youngest and the best looking of the four of them. She spent even more time working out at the MAC than they did, and she had looked terrific. Elaine said it, and Sylvia could not disagree. They carefully avoided the minefield discussion about who might be the next to fall and shifted the conversation to changes in furniture and decorations. The Meijers had kept the roll-playing grand piano, but almost everything else was new. "What" said Elaine, "did you do with all of your old stuff? We have so much of it, but I don't really want to hold a garage sale."

"Oh. No. I couldn't face that either. We gave some of it to the JCC, and the rest is stacked up in the garage. There's a marvelous auctioneer who will come to the house, pick up all that stuff and auction it off at his place. If there's any profit, he just sends you a check. Here, look in the garage. I'll show you. It's just waiting for him."

The first slot in the garage had Sylvia's Mercedes. The second slot had Irv's Jaguar. The third slot was packed with boxes filled with books and household appliances including their first toaster, their second toaster, their first toaster oven, their second toaster oven, their third toaster oven and all the generations of Microwave ovens. There were odds and ends of furniture including a love seat of which Irv had once said "must have seemed like a good idea at the time."

Elaine gave it all an appraising and almost lustful eye. It was all wonderful stuff, but then she forced herself to remember that she didn't know what to do with the stuff she had already. "Discipline, girl", she thought, but there was something that caught her eye, and she kept coming back to it.

"Isn't that" she pointed at a frame sticking up between two chairs, isn't that the needlework that used to hang in the hallway next to the dining room? Little Red Riding Hood?"

"Oh, sure," said Sylvia. "We took it down to make a place for the Chagall I gave Irv for his birthday, and now I'm supposed to take it to the 'Home'. Apparently someone decided that there is some kind of value to these things, and they're going to have a fundraiser. Why, would you like it?"

"Well," Elaine was a little embarrassed. "I would. I always thought it was really cute. When I see it I think of my grandchildren. It would be great in the room they use when they come to visit. They love all the fairy tales."

"Well", said Sylvia, "It has no meaning at all for me. You know, Zaylie made it. God knows, she was with us forever." Sylvia sighed and shrugged a little. "But she was never really like us. I tried to get her to go shopping with us or to go out to a concert. But she seemed mostly to live in her own world. In some ways it is as though she was never here, and yet sometimes I miss her."

"Why shouldn't you have it? Go ahead. It's yours!" Of course, Elaine offered to pay for it.
"Of course you cannot pay me," said Sylvia. "After all, you are my friend." She stressed the "are" and held it for a long time. "If you want to make a contribution to the Home for it, feel free." She pulled it out from its place between the two chairs. "Well, on second thought, you could take me to lunch," and she handed it to Elaine. "And, I'll make a contribution, too, so neither of us has to feel guilty."
"That's a deal" said Elaine. "Where shall we go?" As they took the framed piece out to Elaine's car, this year's red Lexus, which looked almost exactly like last year's red Lexus, they talked about places along Orchard Lake Road where they might combine a really nice lunch with some much needed shopping.

And then they walked back into the house, eager for the beginning of the Passover.